THE MALTESE INCIDENT

Russell F. Moran

The Maltese Incident

Coddington Press

Copyright © 2018 by Russell F. Moran

Printed in the United States of America

ISBN (Print) 978-0-9990003-2-8

ISBN (Ebook) 978-0-9990003-3-5

This book is a work of fiction. The characters, names, incidents, dialogue, and plot are the products of the author's imagination or are used fictitiously. Any resemblance to actual persons or events is purely coincidental.

www.morancom.com

DEDICATION

This book is dedicated to the men and women of the United States Navy.

ACKNOWLEDGEMENTS

As always, I thank my wife, Lynda, for her attentive reading, rereading, and editing of my many drafts, and for laughing at my jokes. I also thank my friend and editor, John White, for his keen editorial eye. And I especially thank my readers, many of whom are a constant source of inspiration and encouragement for me.

AUTHOR'S NOTE

You will find a **Cast of Characters** after the last chapter of the book. It can be frustrating to come across a character on page 150, who you first met on page 20, especially if you've put the book down for a few days. I've seen this done in Russian literature, and I happily add a cast of characters to *The Maltese Incident* as well as my other novels.

The Maltese Incident

CHAPTER ONE

"What the hell was that?" I yelled to First Officer Jim Valente.

"Beats me, captain. I've never seen anything like it."

I'd never seen anything like it either. My gut told me that I was about to start a weird journey. My gut was right.

A few minutes ago, we were steaming through the beautiful Azores when the world turned upside down, for me and everyone else aboard. It was a beautiful April evening with a sky full of stars and a half-moon. I had just chatted with the captain of a yacht off my starboard side about 300 feet away. Based on what the captain of the yacht said, we were both headed for Lisbon, Portugal. At 9:13 p.m., the *Maltese* was suddenly bathed in bright sunlight—at night. We felt a strange rumbling sensation along the hull below the waterline, as if we steamed over submerged logs. After two minutes, nighttime returned, and the rumbling stopped. My weird journey had begun.

***

I grabbed the microphone for the PA system and announced, "General quarters, general quarters, all hands man your battle stations."

"Captain Harry," First Officer Valente said, tapping me on the shoulder. "This isn't a warship. I suggest you make another announcement."

"Oh, right," I said. My Navy years just came back to me. I pressed down the speaker key and made a new announcement.

"Good evening everyone, this is Captain Harry again. I just realized that I'm not running a warship, so please ignore my command to man your battle station, unless your battle station is a barstool. The reason for my sudden burst of nonsense is obvious—we just experienced something weird, insanely weird. First Officer Valente and I are checking all our systems to see if we can figure out what happened. I'll keep you informed."

Jim Valente and I put every system on the ship through a series of tests. What else was there to do? We were trying to figure out what just happened and also checking to see if anything on the ship had changed. I wasn't happy with what we discovered. The starlit sky was now pitch black, and the half-moon was nowhere to be seen. The yacht off to starboard was no longer there. At the moment of our bizarre incident I told Valente to take a fix, an automatic thing for me to say. As I learned in the Navy, anytime something out of the ordinary happens, you take a navigational fix. You don't think about it, you just do it, like saying "God bless you" when somebody sneezes.

"We lost GPS, captain," Valente said after he tried to take a fix. "I can't locate one satellite."

"Radio that yacht to see if we can get a fix from him."

"He doesn't answer, captain. He's not there anymore."

I grabbed the radio microphone. This time I didn't order my passengers to man their battle stations.

"Mayday, mayday, mayday. Any vessel, any vessel, this is the American ship *Maltese*. Come in please."

Mayday is the internationally recognized code for an emergency, and I figured we sure as hell had one.

"Mayday, mayday, mayday. Any vessel, any vessel, this is the American ship *Maltese*. Come in please." I repeated it five times.

No response. We were alone. God knows where, but it was only us.

***

The *Maltese* is a 920-foot ship owned by Malta Investments and which serves the company as its corporate cruise ship. Everybody calls me Captain Harry, including my crew. The *Maltese* can carry 2,900 passengers, but this cruise was a VIP event and only 950 passengers were aboard. The passengers were mainly executives and a few wealthy clients of Malta Investments. I was impressed by the people from Malta ever since I first joined the company. A cruise ship may sound like an extravagant investment, even for a successful company like Malta, but the ship wasn't just for fun and entertainment. Malta donates 100 percent of the net proceeds to a preselected charity for each cruise. This cruise supported children's cancer research. In a world of selfishness, it's a pleasure to work for people who care about something other than themselves. Along with a crew of 35, I run the ship, or I thought I did. I retired from the Navy last year at age 40, young for a retiree, but I started my naval career at age 18 when I went to Annapolis, so I got in 22 years. I liked the Navy, actually I loved it, but after almost getting killed I decided to give civilian life a try. My wife's death from cancer also told me I needed a change in my life, a life in which Nancy played a big part. We had no kids, so I was alone.

In the Navy I was a destroyer captain and I got a reputation among Navy brass that I liked going into combat. That, of course, was bullshit. I never enjoyed combat, but I never avoided it either. So, I was constantly deployed to hot spots around the world. After what just happened to the *Maltese*, I miss the relative safety of naval combat. At least I knew what was coming at me. I went to flight school three years ago, figuring I'd get a carrier command, and who knows, maybe make admiral. That all changed, of course, when I retired.

"Is everything okay, Harry?" Randy Borg asked as he stepped onto the bridge. Randy, or Randolph, is the CEO of the Malta Investments, the company that owns the *Maltese*. He's the guy who hired me and he's my boss, as well as a good friend. I like Randy and I appreciate his attention to detail. You can't run a company as successful as Malta without focusing on details. But he leaves running the ship to me.

"Sure, Randy, everything is just great. I haven't the foggiest fucking idea where we are, how we got here, or where we're going. The only way I'm able to communicate is like we're doing now—talking face to face. We've got a problem, Randy, a big one. All stations have reported, and we sustained no damage, thank God, but we seem to be in the middle of nowhere. I know you don't expect to hear that from the ship's captain, but it's the truth. We're alone in the ocean."

Randy peppered me with a list of questions, the answers to which didn't make him happy. My answers didn't make me happy either.

"Harry, we need to have a meeting of everyone on the ship. Our passengers and crew are entitled to know what's going on. Let's make it for 9 a.m. tomorrow. I want you to conduct the meeting."

***

The following morning Randy and I stood at the entrance to the dining room to greet each of the guests. The list included not only executives and board members of Malta Investments, but also rich clients who invested heavily with Malta. They paid through the nose for this cruise, and even though it was for charity, they were entitled to know what happened. Any of the crew who weren't on watch were also at the meeting. Randy and I figured that it was best to be straight with the audience and talk about our strange circumstance without holding anything back. After breakfast, I stood before the group. I figured the occasion called for it so I wore my full dress white uniform. I wanted everybody to know that I was in charge and on top of the situation. Little did they know that I was as clueless as them.

After everyone was seated I called the meeting to order. We gathered in the main dining room overlooking the sea, which normally provided a beautiful view, but something was wrong. It was daylight, but the atmosphere had a murky quality to it, reminding me of skim milk. At least the sea was calm, without a ripple. Weather reports the night before called for a sunny and cloudless sky, with a brisk wind and choppy seas. But the sky was overcast, the sea was flat as a lake, and there was no wind. Just a few more things about our circumstance that weren't adding up.

***

"Good morning everybody," I said. "Well, we're here to celebrate having an ocean all to ourselves."

I figured that would get a few laughs.

It didn't.

"Randy Borg asked me to be totally frank with you folks, and that's exactly what I will be. But please don't call me Frank; the name's still Harry."

Again, no laughs.

"We're lost. There's no other way to put it. But hey, I've been in worse circumstances at sea. At least nobody's shooting at us."

That brought a couple of chuckles, but I think those people were trying to be polite. I could see why standup comedians spend so much money on psychotherapy.

"I'm going to review our situation, our bizarre situation. I'll be calling on people who wish to comment or share an idea. And I *want* you to weigh in. You people are smart, so I expect that some good ideas are floating around out there. I have one request—no bullshit please. Tell it like it is or how you perceive it. Okay, let me review our weird circumstance.

"Last night, on April 17, we encountered a situation best described as strange. At 9:13 p.m., right after dinner, the dark sky turned to daylight, which lasted for two minutes. During that time the ship rumbled like it was going aground. When the darkness returned, everybody, myself included, ran for a rail to see what was going on. Because it was night, there wasn't much to see. A yacht was on our starboard side, maybe 300 feet from us. After the incident, however, there was only darkness—the yacht simply wasn't there. We sent messages to the boat, but we got no response. I also sent a message to our radio contact in Portugal, about 1,200 nautical miles away. Lisbon, Portugal, was our destination as you know, and I was in continuous radio contact with them, most recently five minutes before the strange event. Lisbon was silent. I then tried to contact New York. No response. Miami—ditto; Washington D.C.—the same. Again, I apologize for ordering you all to your battle stations. After I came to my senses, I figured it was time to declare an emergency to anybody with a radio receiver. I grabbed the radio microphone and yelled the international distress signal, 'Mayday, mayday, mayday. This is the American ship *Maltese*, come in please.'

"I tried that five times. Bottom line, folks, is that I had no way to communicate with any vessel or land location. We tested our radio and it works, both for sending and receiving. At least it works for sending messages from one part of the ship to another. We tried to establish a GPS navigational fix, but after 40 minutes of trying we couldn't locate one satellite. So here we are. I know that you people expect the captain to supply answers, and you have every right to. But I began this talk by telling you that I would be straight with you, and the straight truth is that I don't know what happened.

"Any questions?"

Meghan Johnson, vice president of operations, raised her hand. I grabbed for my glass of water. Ever since Nancy died four years ago, I hadn't thought much about the opposite sex. Maybe the pain of losing her made me scared to fall for another woman. But any time I looked at Meghan Johnson, my heart started pounding. We first met a few days ago when I stood at the bottom of the stairway to welcome passengers aboard. After that, any time I saw her I couldn't help but stare. I estimate that she's about 5'10," with medium length blond hair and the most beautiful blue eyes I've ever seen. She had an athletic body, almost like a gymnast, especially her shapely legs and firm butt. She was striking, and she struck me—hard.

"Wadda you got, beautiful?" I said.

I figured if I dropped into wiseass mode it would relax me and stop me from sweating so much. I drew a deep breath and took a sip of water. I couldn't believe I just called a senior executive "beautiful," true as it may be.

"I've got a question, handsome," Meghan Johnson said, chuckling.

Holy shit, she called me handsome. Suddenly I didn't feel like a 40-year-old sea captain. I felt like a 12-year-old boy who just got his first hard-on. I took another sip of cold water.

"When did you realize that the sky had changed?" Meghan asked.

"Here's where things got totally weird, Ms. Johnson (I switched out of wise-ass mode and decided to be polite). When the sun came up this morning it wasn't normal daylight, if you define daylight as the light cast by a risen sun. The sky was light, but a gloomy kind of light. We found ourselves and our ship inside what looks like a gigantic cave, almost too gigantic to describe. And that's where we've been since *the incident.'* We're in a location that doesn't appear on any chart. If we look up, we can see a cloud cover that almost looks like a roof. The sun isn't visible, but it rises and sets—as if it's behind a screen. We know it rose this morning, but we didn't see the sun itself. I steamed around for a while trying to get a bearing, but I couldn't find out where the hell we were without any normal navigational aids including our electronics. We have an inertial navigation system, but our charts aren't right. There should be land off to starboard, but there's only open ocean."

"Harry, please review for us what you found on sonar," Randy Borg said.

"Our sonar can detect the sea bottom to a depth of about 1,000 meters, or 3,280 feet. We can't detect a bottom, so we know we're in deep water, beyond 3,280 feet. According to our sonar readings before the incident as well as our chart, we had 1,800 feet under us."

"Captain Harry, how much fuel do we have and how far can it get us?" Meghan Johnson asked.

Her blouse was slightly open at the neck, showing a breathtaking view of sun-tanned cleavage. I wiped some sweat off my brow.

"It's comforting to have an operations VP aboard to keep me honest," I said. "The answer won't make anybody happy. With the amount of fuel aboard, we can cruise for no more than 600 nautical miles. I had planned to top off our tanks in Lisbon, but that never happened as we all know. Right now, we're slowly steaming to see if we can find land."

"What about food, Harry? Can you update us?" asked Randy Borg.

"The breakfast we just ate was pleasant, but we're running low on food," I said. "Carlos, our chef, told me that we'll need to invade our flash frozen stores within a few days. We intended to replenish our stock when we got to Lisbon, but of course that didn't happen. We hope that we'll find a source of food on that land we're heading for."

"Okay, the meeting's over, folks," Randy Borg said. "We'll assemble again as a group when we have more information for you. If you have any questions or concerns, please call me or Captain Harry."

***

A day went by and nothing had changed. The same milky sunlight, the same calm ocean, and the same ignorance of where we were. I ordered the engine room to give us eight knots, a fuel-conserving speed. We steamed slowly, looking for land.

"Captain Harry, may I see you for a moment?" Meghan Johnson asked, knocking on the door to the bridge.

"Sorry, I'm busy. You'll have to come back later." Of course, I didn't say that. What I meant to say was, "Oh my God, you look gorgeous." Instead I said, "Sure," after I cleared my throat, "step into my office."

"You can take a break, Jim," I said to the officer on deck. "I'll take the watch from here, not that I have any idea what I'm watching." I did know what I was watching, and it was Meghan Johnson.

"So, what's up, Ms. Johnson?" I said, after taking a swig of cold water. "I hope I didn't embarrass you the other day by calling you beautiful. It just slipped out because you are, well, beautiful."

"I just wanted to say that I found your comment touching," Meghan said. "You took my breath away. You're quite good-looking yourself, captain. Ever since I came aboard I can't help staring at you."

"Are you flirting with me, Ms. Johnson?"

"Yes, I thought you'd never notice. Please call me Meg."

Oh my God. She admitted that she was flirting with me. I glanced at a bulkhead where a defibrillator hung, figuring my heart might need it.

"I hope I didn't upset your husband or boyfriend or whoever that guy is who's constantly at your side."

"He's Phil Jackson, my aide. He looks older, but he just graduated from college. Oh, and I'm not married. You picked a cute way to coax that information out of me."

I said nothing; I just stared into her eyes.

"I'm sorry, Harry, I don't know why I had to share that information. I'm embarrassed."

"Don't be embarrassed, Meg. Maybe you shared that information because you didn't want me to feel uncomfortable talking to you."

"Why would you feel uncomfortable talking to me, Harry?"

"Can I tell you a secret?"

"Sure, Harry. What's your secret?"

"Well, with my loud mouth and my Navy-trained 'command presence,' few people ever spot my little secret—I'm shy as hell." I felt like a little boy kneeling in the booth for my first confession. "Bless me father for I have sinned…"

"I actually spotted that in you, Harry. I even noticed you blush, which I find charming. Now that you've told me your secret, do you still feel shy?"

I took a sip of water and mumbled something inane which I really can't recall. All I noticed was the scent of her perfume.

She moved closer to me to pick some lint off my shirt. I think she just used that as an excuse to come closer. The perfume and the warmth of her body almost made me pass out.

"Now, what was it you wanted to see me about?" I stammered, barely able to catch my breath.

"I forget," Meg said as she took a deep breath. "Oh, yeah. I want to talk to you about breaking our group down into committees."

"I was really hoping that you wanted a business meeting."

"Wise guy," Meg said with a laugh. "Let's take care of business."

I just smiled, reached over, and whisked some hair from her forehead. She grabbed my hand in both of hers and held it against her face, never once taking her eyes off mine. I was no longer feeling shy. Meg cleared her throat, as if to announce that she was changing the subject. As she spoke she continued to hold my hand.

"Here's what I recommend," Meg said. "Randy is definitely the boss, but I can tell that he looks to you for leadership. He's a great guy, but he'd be the first to tell you that he's not a hands-on manager. Back at the office, he relied on me and a few other key executives. So, it's obvious that you're the boss, and the big boss thinks so too. I suggest that you appoint four committees. It will be Randy's decision, of course, but he'll do just about anything that you recommend. I think that the committees should include: First, a lookout committee. We should have recorded notes and photos of anything that a lookout sees; second, a physical plant committee, which means anything involving the ship. You will head that committee, of course; third, a good and welfare committee, which will tend to the various needs of those aboard; and last but not least, a food committee.

It's important that we should have a separate committee addressed to each issue. You will serve as member *ex officio* of each committee, and you'll combine or create new committees as needed. So, what do you think? Hey, Harry, did you hear anything I said?"

"Yeah, something about committees—I think."

I was beginning to feel like I was in the fourth grade when a pretty girl sat at the desk next to me.

Meg laughed. "Yes, it was about committees. We can go over it later."

"I wasn't paying attention because I can't take my eyes off you," I said. "I think that you're beautiful, and I also think that your perfume is driving me insane." Forget what I said about my shyness.

"You really are a charming guy, Harry. I had heard that about you, but now that I'm talking to you in person I can see how that's an accurate description—charming."

I glanced over at the bulkhead to make sure the defibrillator was still there.

"How's this for an idea, Meg? Randy and I dropped that 'dinner with the captain' tradition because of the incident, so how about we replace it this evening with Meg and Harry have dinner? We can talk about committees and stuff."

"Don't I get a formal invitation?" Meg teased.

"Here's your formal invitation." I leaned forward and kissed her.

"In that case, I graciously accept," Meg said, letting out a deep breath.

My secret—that I'm shy—was becoming a secret even to me. For some reason I don't feel shy around Meg Johnson.

CHAPTER TWO

I'm too old to think in terms of "the man of my dreams." Hell, I'm the operations vice president of one of the most successful firms on Wall Street. I have an MBA from Harvard and I've carved out a great career for myself, unencumbered by a partner. Until this weird incident the ship went through, I was happy and contented with my life.

Bullshit. I'm not too old to think about the man of my dreams, and I'm far from being contented with my life. I'm only 35, and I have to admit that I'm in pretty good shape. So, if I'm 35, why do I feel like an adolescent school girl? I've had boyfriends before, but I was feeling different around this guy.

Everybody aboard likes Captain Harry. They like his quick sense of humor and a demeanor that is just plain friendly. He's tall, over 6 feet, crazy handsome, with wavy black hair, a slightly crooked nose, and a devilish twinkle in his sky-blue eyes. Yes, everybody likes him, and so do I—a lot.

I've had my eye on him since we first came aboard. He stood at the foot of the stairway that led up to the ship and greeted every passenger as if they were old friends. As I walked up him, he looked at me and winked. We shook hands, and I noticed that he held onto mine a few moments longer than you would expect from a casual handshake.

"Hi, I'm Meghan Johnson, Vice President of Operations."

Why the hell did I say that, as if he's supposed to give a damn about my title? The more I think about it, the more I'm convinced that I said that to put him in his place, to let him know that I'm a hot-shit executive, and I'm not here to play games.

"Nice dress," he said, smiling. I don't think he caught my title, or if he did, I don't think he cared. Suddenly I lost all interest in trying to impress him with my executive position. He liked my dress. At the time, that was the only important thing.

I looked at his left hand. No wedding ring. That really didn't mean anything. Some men who are on the prowl leave their wedding ring home. But the band always leaves a mark on the ring finger, especially on a man who obviously spends a lot of time outdoors, which results in a drop-dead gorgeous suntan. Where was I? Oh, yes, I came close to asking him to hold his left hand out, so I could examine it more closely. What the hell am I doing? I thought. I finally realized that I was spending an inappropriate amount of time with him. So, I just told him that it was a pleasure to meet him and continued up the stairs. When I got to the top I glanced down and stole another look at him. As if I wasn't embarrassed enough, he looked back at me and winked again.

As soon as I got to my room I dialed Randy Borg's number and told him that, as operations VP, I'd like to see the resumes of the ship's officers. He said that it was a job for the human resources department. I quickly reminded him that our HR manager wasn't on the cruise, so I'd help fill in that role. Sometimes, when I want something, I can be completely full of shit. I went to his room immediately and he gave me the file full of resumes.

"What's the big rush, Meg?" Randy said.

"You know me, Randy," I said. "I like to keep all our ducks in a row."

Especially tall, handsome ones.

Before I even got back to my room I flipped through the resumes till I got to Captain Harry's. "Marital status: single."

The day after the weird night/day incident, Harry called me "beautiful" in front of a room full of people. A day after that I asked Harry if we could meet to discuss some committee ideas I had. We met on the bridge. We talked about my committee ideas, but I really don't recall what we said or concluded. All I remember was kissing Harry. I still remember it. I'll never forget it.

I decided to look at his personnel file in more detail, beyond just "marital status." I saw that he was a widower, his wife having died of cancer. I then looked at his career background.

Wow, I thought, in addition to being good-looking, Harry is one accomplished guy. Besides reading his file, I Googled his name and found a ton of articles about him. This was before our ship lost all communication ability including the Internet. Harry graduated from Annapolis and went on to a career in the Navy. At the young age of 36 he had his own command, a destroyer. Harry mustered out of the Navy with the rank of full captain. He won all sorts of medals for valor. He was 40 years old, which would make him 41 now, just six years older than me.

Besides being impossibly handsome, Harry is just plain fun to be with. What I can't get out of my mind is that I kissed him. And I want to kiss him more. I looked at my watch. It was one hour until we got together for dinner. I took a shower and put on a fresh dress. It's a bit short and has a plunging neckline. Am I crazy acting like this? I thought. Yes, I'm crazy about him.

***

Meg and I met in my private captain's dining room. To celebrate the occasion, I wore my full dress uniform. Meg took my breath away, as she's done before. She wore a dress that highlighted her gorgeous body. That, combined with her perfume, made me stumble over my words.

"That's a drice mess," I said.

"Do you mean a nice dress, Harry?"

"Yeah, that too."

I'm lost at sea, having no idea what to do about it, and my mind has gone into 14-year-old love-struck boy mode. The entire ship looks to me for guidance and leadership, and all I can think about is the beautiful woman I'm with. She's not just a babe, which she definitely is; she's got a brain, a big brain. She also has proven leadership skills because of her job. Hey, she can help me to do my job.

I'm good at coming up with rationalizations to make me feel better about what's going through my mind. My real thoughts consisted of doing all kind of things that have nothing to do with committee assignments.

***

Harry couldn't have been more charming. He even wore his full-dress captain's uniform. Dare I tell him that I've been doing research on him? Dare I congratulate him on a successful naval career and his war hero status? I've dated plenty of men who couldn't stop talking about themselves. Harry is different. If you asked him about himself, he'd probably say, "Just call me Harry."

After dinner we walked outside onto the catwalk surrounding the bridge. The air was wondrously fresh, unlike the murkiness of the daytime, the kind of air that makes your lungs come alive.

"We never did finish our discussion of my committee ideas," I said. I put my hands on his chest just to let him know that I was half-kidding. The last thing I wanted to talk about was my committee plan.

"So, what do you think, Harry?"

"I think I'm crazy about you, Meg."

"What a coincidence," I said. "I was about to say that I'm pretty crazy about *you*."

Things happen fast when you're lost at sea.

CHAPTER THREE

Three days later, Meg and I walked along the deck performing our agreed routine to visit the four lookouts at least once a day. We were spending more and more time together, and I began to imagine Meg as my unofficial executive officer. When she suggested that we inspect the lookout stations together I agreed immediately. If it meant being close to her, I'd agree to anything. Meg carried a clipboard to make our appearance together look official. She moved closer and grabbed my hand.

"Last night was unbelievable, honey," she said softly.

"Well, if you don't believe it we'll have to do it again tonight."

"Sounds like a perfect idea, captain. I'll take that as a direct order."

"I have a confession," I said.

"And what is it you want to confess?"

"I love you, Meg."

"Oh my God, Harry. I love you too."

We hugged for what seemed like an eternity. Not a bad way to spend eternity.

We continued walking and approached the first lookout station.

"Hey, Harry, maybe we should do these lookout visits separately. We're spending so much time together that people are starting to talk."

"So what if they talk? What are they going to say: 'I wonder if Meg and Harry are an item?' So what? Last I checked we're both single. It's not like we're cheating on our spouses. Who cares if we're together a lot? Hell, I don't think we're together *enough*."

Meg grabbed me by my shirt and led me behind a bulkhead on the main deck. She put her arms around my waist.

"You're right, Harry. We're single. We're not married to anybody, including each other. We make love because we're in love, but we're single. Does that all work for you, handsome?"

"Are you proposing marriage to me, Meg? Isn't the guy supposed to do that?"

"I think you hit the tradition right on the head, Harry. So, what are you going to do about it?"

"Will you marry me, Meg?"

"Do you mean it, Harry? You're such a wiseass I can't tell when you're kidding or not."

"Yes, I mean it, Meg. I love you. Marry me. That's an order."

"I thought you'd never ask. The answer is yes."

Meg dropped her clipboard to the deck as we caressed.

So just like that, Meg and I were engaged. Since the ship went through whatever it went through, our lives have been turned upside down. We're lost, and I'm the captain, the guy who's supposed to have the answers, but I don't. I should feel horrible, but I don't. So here I am, lost at sea, and I've never been happier. I'm going to marry a wonderful woman. We'll make a great life together, wherever the hell we are.

"But we need to think about a few things," I said. "Number one, I don't have an engagement ring to give you. Secondly, where the hell will we go on our honeymoon? And third, and this is a big one, who will officiate at our wedding? I'm the captain, so I can marry people, but that's other people, not myself."

"I have the perfect solution, Harry. Forget the ring. You're an expert sailor who knows how to tie a knot. String will do just fine—you can give me a new one every day. As far as a honeymoon, hey, we're on a luxury cruise ship. And about who will officiate, I've got just the person. You know that short redhead, Maureen O'Malley? She's a part time village clerk where she lives on Long Island. She's as official as you can get on this ship."

"So, let's set a date," I said. "We don't need a few months to figure out a guest list and find a catering hall."

"Why don't we ask Randy to make the announcement at our next meeting, and we'll get married at the following one?" Meg suggested.

My parents are proud of me and the stuff I've accomplished. My mother is always prattling on at their country club about "my Harry." If they met Meg, they'd flip out. Sounds trite, but I wish they were here, wherever the hell 'here' is. If we ever figure out a way to get back to where we came from, I want to have a big wedding. I think Meg will want that too.

***

"Captain Fenton, please. Captain Fenton to the bridge," the first officer said. His voice was strained.

Meg and I interrupted our wedding plans and went to the bridge. First Officer Jim Valente was on watch. He also served as one of the lookouts, so our inspection plans didn't change.

"What's up, Jim? You sounded upset about something," I said as we stepped onto the bridge.

"Captain Harry, you won't fucking believe this. Please pardon my language, Ms. Johnson. I felt a sudden movement of the ship. Did you feel it?"

"Yes, I did but I thought it was a wave. So, what are you so concerned about?"

"I looked at sonar and the bottom camera and saw the biggest fish I've ever seen in my life."

"Are you sure it wasn't a whale?" I asked. "We've seen a few of them recently."

"Well, even if it was a whale, the thing was gigantic. Here's a photo I took while part of the thing was still under us."

"My God," I said, "I've never seen anything so big, but its fins don't look like any whale I've ever seen. It's some kind of fish, not a whale—but what kind of goddam fish?"

I showed the photo to Meg.

"How close to us was that thing?" Meg asked.

"I'd say no more than 50 feet," Valente said.

"What the hell was he looking for, a back scratch?" I wondered aloud.

"Bridge, Lookout One. Bridge, Lookout One."

Meg was standing next to the microphone so she responded. "This is the bridge, go ahead Lookout One." Meg has such an easy way to take command of a situation. Meg—my fiancée.

"Check out the port side forward about 200 feet," lookout one shouted.

"Holy shit," the three of us said in unison. We were looking at a dorsal fin protruding about 10 feet into the air.

"Should I steer the ship toward the fin, captain?"

"No way in hell. Colliding with that monster will be like hitting a reef."

"Lookout One, this is Captain Harry. Did you take a photo of that thing?"

"Yes, sir. I got five pictures."

"Make sure you transfer the files to the computer on the bridge when you get off watch. Put them in a file I just created called 'Big Fish.' "

"Holy shit, look at that," yelled Lookout One.

I thought briefly of renaming the *Maltese* to "*Holy Shit*."

The fish had just breached, and its entire body was out of the water. Jim was right, the thing was humongous. When it landed in the water it created a huge wave.

Randy Borg came stumbling through the doorway to the bridge.

"Harry, what the hell was that turbulence all about?"

I showed Randy the photos of our giant aquatic friend.

"I recommend a meeting for all personnel tomorrow in the main dining room, Randy. I'm sure others have seen this monster and I don't want people freaking out."

"Hey, Harry," Meg said. "What about the big announcement we want Randy to make?"

"Oh, right. Meg and I are getting married and I'd like you to be my best man."

I don't know what "beaming" looks like, but it's how I felt.

"Also," I said, "we'd like you to make the announcement, maybe at tomorrow's meeting. Our wedding plans will give us something else to talk about besides a giant fish."

"That's fabulous," Randy yelled. "Congratulations you two." He walked over to Meg and gave her a kiss on the cheek and gave me a bear hug.

"I want to make the wedding announcement before we show the photos of the monster," Randy said. "I think it will be good for morale."

CHAPTER FOUR

Randy Borg stood in front of the audience and took the microphone. The meeting was in the ship's main dining room because it accommodated all guests and crew of the *Maltese* except for those on watch.

"Today we're going to discuss some strange things." Randy said. "We all know about the bizarre occurrence a few days ago. But before we discuss the odd incident, I first want to announce some great news, some happy news. Captain Harry and our own Meg Johnson are getting married. I have it in strict confidence that they are going to spend their honeymoon on a cruise ship. Maureen O'Malley from our accounting department happens to be Clerk of the Village of Garden City, New York, and as our resident government official she will perform the wedding ceremony. The wedding will take place at our next meeting. Let's hear it for Captain Harry and his lovely fiancée, Meg Johnson."

The crowd stood and gave us a roaring, foot-stomping standing ovation. We may be lost at sea, but at least we're on a ship full of friends.

***

Our wedding day arrived. I wore my formal captain's uniform and Meg wore a light blue gown that she had brought with her for formal dinners. Everybody snapped pictures.

"I want to frame one of these photos and hang it on our wall—next to the giant fish picture."

"You're such a romantic, Harry," Meg said.

Maureen O'Malley, who has a big voice despite her petite size, performed the wedding ceremony. The aging Jake Mendenhall, Senior Vice President for Finance, stood in as Meg's father to give the bride away.

When the wedding ceremony was completed, the waiters opened champagne bottles and poured the bubbly into each person's glass. Randy Borg, in his role as best man, proposed a toast and gave a short speech.

"Ladies and gentlemen, each one of us is consumed by one thing, an obvious thing—we're lost. But despite our quandary, sometimes things turn out well. We're gathered to celebrate, not a sea monster, but Harry and Meg's wedding. They're two of the best people I know, and it delights me that they're now man and wife. I'm also proud that Captain Harry asked me to be his best man. Immediately after our wedding lunch, we'll discuss the strange sightings recently, and look at some photographs. But now, please raise your glass in a toast to our favorite people, Harry and Meg Fenton."

The crowd raised their glasses toward Meg and me when suddenly the ship listed hard to starboard, spilling everybody's champagne on the closest person. I grabbed Meg by the hand and said, "We need to go to the bridge."

"Our guests of honor have suddenly been called away," Randy announced. "Please put your glasses into the nearest receptacle to avoid breakage and stay near any solid object you can grab onto. Everyone please stay here for the meeting, which has just taken on immediate importance. I'm following Captain Harry and Meg to the bridge, so we can figure out what just happened. I'll report to you from there."

"Whatta we got, Jim?" I said to the first officer.

"Our big friend is back, captain, but this time he came even closer. The lurch we all felt was the damn thing bumping against our hull. I think he's in love with the *Maltese*. By the way, congratulations on your wedding. I wish I could have been there."

"Thanks, Jim. It was pretty short, thanks to our monster friend."

"I snapped some pictures with the hull-bottom camera. I transferred the photos to the bridge computer so we can get a good look on the wide screen. Check this out."

Randy Borg had just entered the bridge, and I motioned him over to the computer screen.

"Oh my God," said Randy. "That thing looks like it's half the size of this ship."

"Did you see what was following it?" Meg said. "Three little ones, if you can describe something the size of a school bus as 'little.'"

"I'm going to increase speed a bit and make for shore, which we can finally see on the horizon," I said. "We need to get into shallow waters, assuming I can find a bottom."

"I suggest pinging the sonar, honey," Meg said. "That may keep the big fish away from the ship,"

"And to think that I married you for your looks. Meg's right, Jim, let's set the sonar to ping every 30 seconds. Steer course 340. We don't have reliable charts, but I want to steer visually between those two mountains. The landscape looks flat, and with any luck the depth will be shallow enough to drop the anchor."

"Maybe we can take a real honeymoon ashore, handsome."

"Let's see what kind of wild animals are there first."

"If they're as wild as you, I'm ready, honey," Meg said.

Randy rolled his eyes.

"What speed do you want, captain?" Jim Valente asked.

"Increase it, but to just to nine knots, Jim. We still need to conserve fuel."

"When we drop the anchor, we can do some fishing to replenish our stores," Randy said.

I looked at Meg, who was standing next to me in her wedding dress. We both laughed. Only a short-story writer with a strange sense of humor could have come up with a description of our brief wedding ceremony.

***

I've never been married before, and I expected that Harry and I would have a nicer wedding, one that wasn't upstaged by sea monsters. I'm beginning to realize that everything will look weird from here on out. Like everybody else on this ship, my emotional state goes from fear to upset, but right now, despite our monster fish encounter, I feel great. I just married a wonderful man, and I refuse to let our newlywed happiness wear off. Harry's a positive thinker and so am I. We'll handle this bizarre situation day by day—together. Fuck the sea monsters, as my husband would say.

CHAPTER FIVE

"We can't be the only ship that got hit with this madness," I said. "There's an ocean full of ships cruising to different ports. Can we be the only one?"

Meg was standing watch with me on the bridge.

"You're right," Meg said. "It doesn't make any sense that we're alone with this crap. Other ships may be in danger too, but we don't have a way to warn them."

Being lost at sea is one of those primordial fears that have kept novelists busy since the beginning of the written word. I'm on a ship with over a thousand intelligent people, my new wife being one of the brightest. We have plenty of brains to work on our problem. What bothers the hell out of me is that I don't have any explanation for what happened to us, not a clue. One minute we were steaming along on a beautiful evening; the next minute night turned into day, the ship rumbled, and here we are in an ocean full of giant fish. This disgusting gloomy weather isn't helping my mood. It's after sunrise, but we can't see the sun, or even the light patch above the clouds where it's hiding. A TV weatherman would describe our current climate as "overcast with a chance of rain."

I just recalled that prior to our incident, another ship would be heading our way through the Azores. That big new Norwegian Cruise Line ship, the *Melody of the Seas* was scheduled to leave Manhattan today. I know her captain, a nice guy named Lars Ragnarssen, a perfect name for a Norwegian Cruise Line captain. We had a drink just a couple of weeks ago at a bar near the piers. I remember him saying that the *Melody* would be leaving today. The ship could be tossing off her lines right now.

***

The deep rumbling sound of the ship's horn sounded as the *Melody of the Seas* cast off its lines from the Norwegian Cruise Line terminal at Pier 88 on the West Side of Manhattan. The ship was embarking on a three-week European cruise, its fourth passage. The schedule also called for two days of steaming through the beautiful Azores. The April temperature, despite a cloudless sky, had a slight chill. As the ship steamed slowly down the Hudson River, the public-address system played Frank Sinatra's *New York, New York,* a traditional song played over the loudspeakers of an outbound cruise ship as it passed Manhattan to port.

The *Melody of the Seas* was the newest ship launched by Norwegian Cruise Line. At 230 gross tons and 1,200 feet in length it was the largest cruise ship afloat, although she would probably keep that record for only a few months. The cruise ship industry keeps going for bigger and better. The vessel's 2,747 staterooms accommodated 2,479 passengers and a crew of 2,300.

Captain Lars Ragnarssen has been with **Norwegian Cruise Line** for all his 30-year career. After this cruise he'll have five more trips before retirement. Like many a sea captain, he had mixed feelings about retiring. He always loved the sea, and he had already placed a deposit on 50-foot motor yacht, not exactly a cruise ship, but big enough to get him to the ocean when the yearning hit him. The boat would be berthed in Lars' hometown of Oslo, Norway.

Lars spoke with only a trace of his native Norwegian accent. Captain Lars, as everybody called him, no longer brings his wife to sea with him. He had learned that lesson after an expensive divorce from his fourth wife, who caught him giving private nautical lessons to a passenger in a hot tub. Lars stood just under six feet tall with blond hair, which he encouraged with hair coloring whenever gray asserted itself. At age 55, he had a youthful appearance to compliment his good looks. Rumor had it that many a single woman booked a cruise just to rub elbows with Captain Lars. According to cruise ship tradition, the captain would dine with a different group of passengers every night. Lars' wife, Inga, his fifth, is a stunning beauty who owns a chain of clothing stores. Lars is determined that Inga will be his final marriage. He almost said that to a lovely young American woman who flirted with him one evening. He almost said that, but instead asked if he could buy the lady another drink.

Despite his mutual attraction with good-looking women, Captain Lars took his job as a mariner and ship captain to heart. He knew that the complexities of a giant cruise ship presented countless problems, some life-threatening. Other than heart attacks, falls, swimming pool accidents, and the occasional suicide, his record for passenger safety was unblemished. Long ago, Lars internalized the lessons of *The Titanic*, and of its ill-fated captain, Edward Smith. The story has been told many times in print and on the screen. Lars had read Walter Lord's book, *A Night to Remember*, a dozen times. Captain Smith had allowed himself to be bossed around by the White Star Line brass and ordered a cruising speed much too fast for the iceberg-clogged seas that surrounded the ship. When the lookout spotted the huge iceberg dead-ahead, it was too late to turn the ship. Never would he let the safety of his ship and passengers be compromised by someone else. When he stood on the bridge as captain, the ship was his and he was in command, not some guy at headquarters in a business suit. He liked it that way, and so did the women he dined with.

The Verrazano Bridge glistened in the late afternoon sun as the huge ship steamed under it, gliding out into the Atlantic. Lars thought about his new friend, Captain Harry Fenton, skipper of the *Maltese*, the ship that went missing a couple of days ago. It's always hard to lose a friend, especially when your friend simply disappears.

***

As the *Melody of the Seas* passed the coast of New Jersey to starboard, the First Officer Bob Simmons approached the captain.

"Good evening, sir, I have a message for you."

He handed the captain the printout of a message from the **Norwegian Cruise Line** home office. The letter, from the president of NCL, warned about the dangers of terrorism, and recommended extreme caution. Ever since the *Achille Lauro* was hijacked off Egypt in 1985, security on cruise ships was tight. The events of 9/11 and other prominent terrorist actions over the years made cruise ship management edgy.

Lars looked at Simmons and shook his head.

"Trouble, captain?" Simmons said.

"No, not exactly, Bob. Just another message from the home office warning about terrorism."

"Let me guess, captain. They're worried about the *Maltese Incident.*"

"Yes, they are. After the *Maltese* went missing the cruise line industry will never be the same."

CHAPTER SIX

"Good afternoon, ladies and gentlemen, Shepard Smith here for *Fox News*. I have an update to the story we broke two days ago concerning the cruise ship *Maltese*.

"The ship disappeared while steaming in the Azores, en route to Lisbon, Portugal. No distress signal was heard, and nothing indicated that the ship was in trouble. Submersibles have scoured the sea bottom in the area where the ship went missing, but no debris has been found.

"So far nobody has come up with an explanation of just what happened—or just where the ship is. The unexplained event has become known as the *Maltese Incident*. The *Maltese* is owned by Malta Investments, a huge and successful securities firm. The company uses the ship to entertain clients on charity fund raisers. I'm going to tell you more about the *Maltese* from information given to us by the current board of directors.

"Her skipper is a man well-known in maritime circles. Captain Harold Fenton, or Captain Harry as everybody knows him, is a graduate of the United States Naval Academy. He saw action in the Persian Gulf as commanding officer of the *USS Bentley*, a destroyer. Captain Harry received a chest wound and facial injuries in an encounter with Iranian gunboats, earning him the Purple Heart. He was also awarded the Navy Cross for valor. After his military service he went back to sea as a captain on private cruise ships. Besides his seagoing expertise, he's known for his sense of humor and colorful language. From everything I've read about him, Captain Harry's quite a guy, liked by anyone who's met him. But now he's missing, along with the *Maltese* and all her crew and passengers.

"We'll bring you updates to this still-breaking story as we receive them."

CHAPTER SEVEN

"Sonar shows 300 feet, captain," said the first officer Jim Valente.

"Another mind-blower," I said. "A few yards to seaward and we couldn't spot bottom, now we're in 300 feet of water. Let me know as we get shallower. Give me 25-foot intervals."

Meg walked onto the bridge carrying a tray with our lunch. Meg and I were standing watch together.

"What have you got for us, honey?"

"Guess—fish. We ran out of filet mignon. If we send a scouting party ashore, maybe they can pick up what we can't find at sea. Chef Carlos told me he would love to get his hands on some olive oil so he can perk up the taste of the fish dishes."

"If we find some small game, even better," I said.

"225 feet, captain."

"Very well, slow to five knots and keep the numbers coming."

"What depth are you looking for, Harry?" Meg asked.

"I want 75 feet, enough to give us a comfortable anchorage. Of course, a lot depends on wave activity onshore."

"I wonder why we haven't seen one of those gigantic fish for days," Meg said.

"There's no pattern to it, Meg. They either show up or not. We don't know how to attract them, not that I'd want to. Hey, from the look of things ashore, I think we're going to arrive in a good spot."

"The land looks beautiful, Harry. It looks like an untouched forest. And where did that beautiful sunshine come from? All the time we were at sea it was overcast, but now there isn't a cloud in the sky."

"75 feet, captain," Valente said, "75 and holding."

"Anchor room, this is the bridge, all engines stop," I yelled. "Let go the anchor."

When I was in the Navy, I seldom had to yell. The entire crew was well trained and could take voice orders even when I spoke softly. On this civilian ship, it's different. I yell a lot.

I maneuvered the ship to make sure the anchor was firmly secured.

"All engines back one-third. All stop. All engines ahead one-third. All stop." I felt at home, handling a ship in an anchorage. The anchor was secure in a sandy bottom.

***

For the shore party I picked six men, beside myself, out of 50 volunteers. I chose them for their outdoor experience, including hunting, military background, and the ability to handle a gun. We would go ashore using one of our 25-foot excursion boats. I tapped Dominic Maslow as my second in command. When back on the job, Dominic was the vice president in charge of IT, but he had a lot of experience as a sportsman as well as some solid military background where he saw combat as an Army Ranger.

We were surprised—surprised and happy—to see the island bathed in sunshine, a nice break from the dreary weather at sea.

"Don't forget to make room for me," Meg said, as we entered the meeting room.

"You're not coming, honey. We have no idea what we're going to encounter. I want you here where you're safe."

"Harry, are you telling me I'm not in good physical shape?"

"God no," I had to admit. "You're in wonderful shape. But you're not cut out to be stomping through a jungle."

"And you are? I bet the closest you ever came to a jungle was gardening."

Not even that, actually. I live in a high-rise condo. I was getting an annoying feeling that I was losing the argument to Meg. I can't just give her an order. Well, maybe I can, but she wouldn't obey it so why bother. I tried for one last debate point.

"Hon, we're all going to be heavily armed. It's anybody's guess what kind of animals we'll bump into. We've got to be ready to open fire at a moment's notice to protect ourselves."

Meg reached onto the table and picked up an AR-15, the kind of semi-automatic rifle the ship carries. Without taking her eyes off mine, she pressed the release button and popped the magazine out, which she caught in her left hand. She cradled the rifle under her right arm, inserted a dummy round into the magazine, rammed it back into the rifle, secured it, and chambered the dummy round. The whole process took about 15 seconds. She looked at me the entire time and didn't blink once.

Having lost the argument, I was about to deliver my concession statement when Meg smiled and said,

"Remember, honey, my father was a Marine. He taught his daughter how to handle a gun. Dad wasn't satisfied until I could shoot the balls off a gnat at 30 yards."

I married well.

The rest of the shore party came into the room, led by Randy Borg, who would not be going ashore.

"Captain Harry, I'll let you handle this," Randy said.

"We all thank you for volunteering to go ashore," I said, "including Meg, who's more than good with a firearm. I'll be leading our party and Dom Maslow will be second in command. If I sound military, it isn't just my background speaking, it's because I want to emphasize that discipline will be necessary on this trip. I guess that when you joined Malta Investments, you didn't expect to go exploring islands in search of food.

As you all know, the provisions aboard the *Maltese* are limited, and that's why we're going to explore the land. We don't want to take risks, because we don't know what we'll find ashore. Chef Carlos has given us a shopping list of food that we need. If we discover food in large amounts, we'll launch other boats to help bring the stuff aboard. Among the many things we don't know about this land is what kind of animals inhabit the place. We hope they'll be edible, but they may also be dangerous. You have plenty of guns and ammo. Don't be afraid to use them—for food or for protection. Keep in mind that the *Maltese* was bumped by a huge animal, bigger than any shark we've ever seen. Do we expect to find anything as large on land? We have no idea. Just keep your powder dry."

"Keep your powder dry? You sound just like John Wayne, sweetie. Why don't you start calling me 'little lady.' "

The group cracked up at Meg's comments. She has a way of lightening things up.

"Okay, any questions? Any comments, Dom?"

"I've had a lot of training in searching for food when I was in the Army," Dom Maslow said. "I suggest that you show it to me before you drag anything back to the ship. I'm pretty good at distinguishing between what's edible and what's fatal."

"Good. Speaking of food, we're going to take some of the little remaining meat we have aboard. We'll need it for energy. Chef Carlos put together a few ham and turkey sandwiches. Okay, folks, let's see what's happening ashore."

"Aren't you supposed to say, 'Move Out' or something like that?" my wiseass wife said to her wiseass husband.

***

Dom Maslow took over the controls of the motor launch. I assigned two men to jump off the bow when we hit the beach.

The boat came to a stop on a smooth, sandy bottom, with little wave activity behind us to cause problems. After the two men wrapped a line around a tree, we all dragged the bow onto dry sand. I raised my hand to signal for silence. All we could hear were jungle sounds like a Hollywood adventure movie.

"Sounds pretty harmless to me," I said. "Okay, let's move out."

"Well said, captain," Meg said, slapping me on the shoulder.

"This place looks safe enough," I said, "but let's be careful. Make sure your guns are loaded and be ready to flip off the safety at a moment's notice. Okay, let's walk slowly, look from side to side, and stay alert."

"What you said about that gigantic fish got me thinking, captain," said Rick Ramos. "We should be ready to shoot first and take pictures later."

Ramos worked in the engine room on the *Maltese*. I picked him because he served in the Army. He's a tough little guy who never shuts up.

"Besides photos, we should take notes," I said. "Jot down your impressions and don't worry about editing the content. We can sort it all out later."

"Hey, people," Dom said, "doesn't this ground look amazingly flat. It looks like it was tamped down by a steamroller flattening a path through tall grass."

"Yeah, but it's not uniform like you would expect of something that was flattened," Frank Murphy said. "It looks like uneven footprints and something being dragged."

"Wait, stop," I shouted. "Look ahead of you. Murphy's right, the shapes in the grass look like footprints of an animal—a big animal. Let's keep going. The trail, if that's what you want to call it, bends up ahead."

"Holy shit," yelled one of the men. "What the hell is that?"

"Everybody drop down and speak in a low voice," I said. "Does anybody know what that thing is?"

"That's a *Brachiosaurus,*" Frank Murphy said, "Didn't you guys see *Jurassic Park?*"

I pointed my camera at Meg's face and snapped a photo.

"I got a perfect 'Laura Dern' moment," I said.

"You got a what?" Meg asked.

"You know, like in the movie when Laura Dern, playing a paleontologist, got her first glimpse of a *Brachiosaurus.*"

"*Jurassic Park* was a movie," Maslow said, "this is reality—I think. Hey, Murph, you seem to know a lot about dinosaurs."

"Yeah, it's a sort of hobby of mine. I picked it up from my son."

"So, tell us, Murph, does that big fucker eat people?" Ramos asked.

"No, it's strictly a vegetarian."

"I thought vegetarians were slim," Meg said.

"Murph, call out the name of these critters as we see them," I said, "and don't forget to take pictures."

"Why don't we just send the pics to the ship, captain?" Ramos asked.

"Show me a cell tower and I'll agree with you. For now, just keep the pictures on your phones. We'll download them to the file server when we get back to the ship. Hey, what's that rumbling?"

"Looks like our *Brachiosaurus* friend is being joined by some pals for lunch," Murphy said.

Four gigantic *Brachiosaurs* stomped into view, eating the leaves off tall trees as they walked. One of them stood on its hind legs to reach a high branch, just like in the movie. It must have been 100 feet to the top of its head.

We heard a loud roar in the distance. I couldn't believe what I was seeing and hearing

"Sounds like a bunch of tigers practicing harmony," Rick Ramos said.

"Very funny, Rick," I said. "Whatever sent out that noise was one big animal—with a bad attitude. Hey, everybody crouch down behind this bush."

As we hid ourselves, the animal came into view about 300 feet ahead of us.

"Frank, what is that thing?" Meg said to Murphy in a whisper.

"That, my friends, is a *Tyrannosaurus Rex*, the meanest carnivore that ever existed. He's not coming this way but stay down while he's in view."

"Okay, everybody listen up," I said. "Part of our job is to evaluate this land as a place to live if necessary. From what I see, the vegetation indicates a decent climate, and a lot of those things hanging from trees look edible. The land looks flat enough for building, and we can cut down some of those tall trees for lumber. I see this island as a definite possibility if we need to move off the *Maltese*. I could get used to this place."

"Harry, behind you!" Meg screamed as she raised her rifle, dropped to a knee, and fired three rounds into the torso of a six-foot monster that was charging us.

"What the fuck is that thing?" I yelled to Frank Murphy.

"It's a *Velociraptor*, one of the fiercest dinosaurs that ever lived. They often travel in packs so keep your weapons ready. Just a thought, guys, because there's a lady with us, I suggest that we don't precede every question with 'what the fuck.'"

"Don't worry about it, Murph," Meg said, laughing. "I've heard a lot worse on the trading floor of the New York Stock Exchange."

"Hey, Captain Harry, do you still like it here?" Ramos asked.

"I like it here as long as we've got plenty of ammunition," I said. "Hey, Murph, the animals seem to be skittish around gunfire. Is that my imagination?"

"I have no answer for that other than what we've observed, but it seems logical that animals would be afraid of strange loud sounds. Hey, around loud noises they're no different from a dog, a cat, or a human being for that matter."

As we walked, Meg kept pointing to vegetation that appeared to be edible and asked Dom Maslow for his opinion. She'd then take a photo of the item and make notes on her pad.

"Murph, you're our resident dinosaur maven," I said. "Can you summarize your thoughts for us?"

"Well, captain, besides the obvious fact that we're millions of years in the past, I think we've seen a rewriting of what we know about geologic time. Until today I thought that the *Brachiosaurus* and the *Pterodactyl* coexisted in the late Jurassic period, anywhere from 148 to 154 million years ago. I also know, or I thought I knew, that the *T-Rex* and the *Velociraptor* lived in the late Cretaceous period, from 66 to 75 million years ago. And our giant shark friend, the *Megalodon*, lived in the early Miocene period, and lasted through the end of the Pliocene era, about 2.6 to 23 million years ago. So, we've time travelled anywhere from 2.6 million years to 154 million years. Our scientific studies of the age of the dinosaurs will need to be rewritten."

"Maybe we should call a press conference," Meg said, always the wiseass.

"I don't know about you guys, but I'm willing to call our visit with the monsters a day," I said. "Meg has a list of edible vegetation which we'll gather on our next trip. The boat is only a couple of hundred feet behind us."

"Would that be the boat that's loaded with cartons of meat sandwiches?" Murphy asked.

"Oh shit, I should have thought of that. Let's go. Safeties off your guns."

As we approached the berm over which our boat was located, we heard a riotous commotion of apparently small animals. When we reached the top of the berm we saw about 20 small dinosaurs fighting over the sandwich cartons.

"Looks like we have company for lunch," I said. "What are they, Murph, besides hungry?"

"Some kind of small *raptor*. They're no bigger than chickens but a lot nastier, and from the way they're chowing down on our sandwiches they know how to bite."

"Okay, everybody. Shoot to kill and be careful not to hit the boat."

We all opened fire at the hungry little dinosaurs. Meg casually picked off five of them. The forest behind us erupted with the sound of birds taking flight. Three giant *Pterodactyls* flew down the beach.

"Cease fire," I shouted. "Let's climb aboard and get the hell out of here."

Ramos reached into the boat to retrieve the carcass of what he thought was a dead dinosaur, when it suddenly turned on him and bit his arm. He flung the little animal across the sand, and Meg blasted its head off with one shot.

"Peter, get a tourniquet around that wound," I said to Peter Thompson, who was a medical corpsman when he was in the Marines.

"I want everybody to keep your guns ready as we head to the ship," I said.

I squeezed Meg's knee and leaned over so she could hear me over the roar of the boat engine.

"The next time we're involved in a situation that requires gunfire, I want you at my side."

"I'm always at your side, honey," she said. "Hey, you've got a round chambered and your safety's off. I recommend pointing your barrel into the air, captain."

"Aye, aye, sweetheart."

We pulled up to the *Maltese* 20 minutes later.

"Theresa," Meg yelled to Dr. Theresa Rosario, the only physician on the ship. "We have a man who was bitten by an unknown animal. Use whatever antibiotic you think is appropriate."

Meg and I stood next to the gurney that Ramos was on and I said, "How do you feel, Rick?"

"Great," said Ramos as he winced in pain. "I think I'm the only living person who's been bitten by a dinosaur."

"Dinosaur?" yelled Dr. Rosario and a few others who were close by.

Randy walked into the room.

"We'll explain it all to you at our meeting later, including photos," I said. "It's 2 p.m. by my watch. Can you guys be good to go for a meeting in one hour?"

"I just need to powder my nose," Meg said.

"And clean your gun and count your ammo, if I know the new you," I said.

"Hey, once a Marine brat always a Marine brat."

"Captain Harry, we're all hungry. Could the chef put something together for us?" Murphy said.

"Didn't you guys eat the sandwiches that Chef Carlos prepared for you?" Randy said.

We all laughed.

"We shared our lunch with some uninvited guests, Randy. We'll tell you and everybody about it at the meeting. We're ready to put on a photography show like you've never seen, including our little lunch guests who ate our sandwiches. Please ask the audio/video people to put a big screen in place. We have a lot of pics to show."

***

After we all showered and changed into fresh clothes, we met in the ship's theater to prepare the slide show. I wanted to put things into perspective for the crowd that would soon fill the theater.

"Okay, guys, we're going to hear a lot of questions," I said. "I want you to be wide open and answer honestly. Don't worry about scaring people. We all need to adjust to our new reality."

At 3 p.m. the crowd began to fill up the theater. I walked to the front.

"Good afternoon, everybody," I said. "I'm pleased to introduce our shore excursion team that arrived back aboard an hour ago. By now you've heard all the gossip. What you're about to see and hear will beat the rumors. In the past few weeks we realized that something strange happened to our ship and to us. You're about to find out how strange it is. Before I begin our slide presentation and our narrative, I'd like to introduce Frank Murphy, a securities analyst by day and a strange-animal aficionado after hours. Frank will begin our talk by giving everybody some perspective on the huge fish that's been trying to hump the ship."

"Good afternoon," Murphy said. "Yes, it's true that my hobby is strange animals, specifically dinosaurs. My son got me involved while I led a school trip of his, and I've been a dinosaur nut ever since. From my studies of geologic time, I estimate that we've travelled into the past over 100 million years. From what we saw ashore, I can now tell you that the big fish that seems to have fallen in love with the *Maltese* is a *Megalodon*, a prehistoric shark. You heard me right—I said prehistoric. As I recall from class trips to the Museum of Natural History, the *Megalodon* grew to a size over 60 feet. From the photographs that our people have taken, our visitor was big, even for a *Megalodon*. I suggest that you keep your fingers out of the water."

Nobody laughed.

"I'm now going to ask our excursion leader, Captain Harry, to tell you all about our trip ashore. I'll stand by to help with any dinosaur questions," Murphy said.

Using photographs taken by the group, I told the tale of the *Brachiosaurus*, the *Tyrannosaurus rex*, the *Velociraptor* that charged us, and the nasty little sandwich-eating raptors. I described the rumbling earth caused by the *Brachiosaurs*, the fierce roar of the *T-rex*, and the viciousness of the small raptors.

"We all had to fire our weapons. I'm happy that my wife Meg convinced me to include her in the excursion. She's so accurate with a gun I think the dinosaurs will scatter the next time they see her."

Still no laughs. Everybody seemed stunned by our presentation.

"Ladies and gentlemen," I concluded, "we find ourselves in a different world."

The room was silent.

Meg leaned over and whispered in my ear, "I'm amazed that there are so few questions."

"I think these people are scared, Meg."

"Aren't you?" she said. "It's only been a few hours, and I still can't believe that we were walking among dinosaurs—friggin dinosaurs."

"I've got a question," Randy said. "Harry, our major objective in sending you brave folks ashore was to find additional food sources. Now we find that the land is inhabited by prehistoric monsters. Is there anything we can do to kill those bastards so we can gather some food?"

"Well, given enough firepower, and a large enough group ashore, we can fend off the beasts while we scrounge for food. Dom Maslow said that he identified plenty of edible fruit on the trees and Meg recorded his findings. The dinosaurs appear to be afraid of loud noises like the blast from a gun. If your next question is 'how much is enough?' the answer is that I simply don't know. Dom Maslow can tell you how much ammo a platoon needs when on patrol, but as far as dinosaurs go, all I can say is that I wouldn't tackle a *Tyrannosaurus* with only one of our rifles."

"Is there anything we can do to make the animals friendlier?" Mary Blackwell asked.

"You can just as easily domesticate a rattlesnake, Mary," Frank Murphy said. "The plant-eating dinosaurs, like the *Brachiosaurus*, aren't aggressive, but I wouldn't want one of them to accidentally step on me. As far as the carnivorous dinosaurs, consider the only friendly one a dead one, especially the raptors."

"Do you think any of the dinosaurs may be edible?" Chef Carlos asked.

"Carlos, if you're prepared to cook and taste one," I said, "I'll join you for a meal. One leg from a *Brachiosaurus,* if edible, could feed us all for a few weeks."

Another hand went up. It was Maurice Thurston, one of Malta's wealthier clients.

"Captain Harry," Maurice said, "we've all heard speculation that we may plan to construct a compound ashore at some point. Would you please comment on that, and include the dinosaurs in your remarks."

"Excellent question, Maurice. Yes, some of those dinosaurs are big and mean, but they're not bullet proof. And here's some good news about that. I spoke to Bob Flowers, the VP of Science at Malta, and he said that we store a large supply of sulfur, charcoal, and potassium nitrate aboard, the chemicals used to make the gunpowder we need. Potassium nitrate is actually sodium-free salt, and we have a ton of it. He's figured out how we can make more of those substances, so we'll have all the gunpowder we need. Brilliant Bob has even figured out a simple way to make bullets, using spent shell casings. Not to my surprise, my Marine-trained wife, Meg, picked up all the spent shell casings from our encounters with the dinosaurs."

Meg held up a pillow case and shook it. You could hear empty shells jingling in the bag.

"So, in a long-winded answer to your question, Maurice, yes, the possibility of moving ashore is a workable one, as long as we have a steady supply of ammo. We stock plenty of guns, and even a few hand grenades for anti-terrorism purposes. So that should take care of the dinosaur problem. We may be more of a problem to them than they are to us. If we ever do move ashore, we don't want to live in tents, so I checked the trees, and they all look suitable for making lumber. The prior owner of this ship left a huge supply of building material aboard, including lumber, saws, and cutting tools. We're in the early stages of talking about moving ashore, but I'm asking everybody to keep your thinking caps on. It just may happen. It just may *have to* happen."

As the crowd filed out of the room, Meg leaned over to me and said, "So how do you size up the situation, honey? Maybe we should set up a dinosaur petting zoo on the ship."

"Gimme a kiss, wiseass. We've got some long-range planning to talk about."

CHAPTER EIGHT

After a two-day stay in Southampton, England, the *Melody of the Seas* headed back into the Atlantic and cruised south toward the Azores, after which the ship would dock in Lisbon, Portugal. The Azores is officially named the Autonomous Region of the Azores, one of two autonomous regions of Portugal. It's an archipelago consisting of nine volcanic islands west of the mainland. The scenery from a ship is beautiful—unless your ship disappears.

Captain Ragnarssen announced over the public-address system that there would be a memorial service for the souls aboard the *Maltese* in exactly two hours.

***

"Captain, look at this," Simmons shouted as he stared at his screen. "You're looking at the tail end of the thing. I saw the whole fish and it was a hell of a lot bigger."

Captain Lars leaned over the viewing screen that showed what the camera under the hull recorded.

"My God, that thing is huge. It must be a blue whale. I'm just looking at the tail, but I can see how big it is."

"Whatever it was, it's gone," Simmons said. "Is that the same weird fish we have in photos?"

They felt a lurch, causing Simmons to collide with a bulkhead.

"Are you okay, Bob?" Lars said, handing him a handkerchief to press against his bleeding forehead.

"Are *we* okay is the question, captain," Simmons said. "What do you suppose is next on the agenda?"

Lars picked up a radio and hailed a destroyer steaming nearby.

"*USS Forrest Sherman,* Lieutenant Pierce speaking," came the reply.

"This is Captain Lars Ragnarssen on the *Melody of the Seas.* May I please speak to the captain of the *Forrest Sherman.*"

"I'll call him to the bridge, sir. We're still picking ourselves up off the deck after being rammed by something."

"When did that happen, lieutenant?"

"No more than two minutes ago, captain. It felt like we were hit by a whale."

"Did you get a look at it?" Lars asked as he wiped sweat off his brow.

"I didn't see her, but the quartermaster of the watch saw the thing. He said it was bigger than any whale he'd ever seen. I think he exaggerated a bit, but the point is it was one big fish. It didn't really ram us, it just brushed against our hull from what we can tell. If it rammed us we wouldn't be here. Our captain wants to speak to you."

"Captain Jim Langdon speaking. Are you Captain Ragnarssen of the *Melody of the Seas?*"

"Yes, Captain Langdon. Please call me Lars. It looks like we picked the same monster to bump into."

"Monster is the word, Lars. I'm heading toward shore now until we can figure out what the hell happened. There's an anchorage that can accommodate a big ship like the *Melody.* I wish I was aboard your ship on a cruise, so I could let you worry about our Moby Dick friend."

Both ships dropped anchors in a natural harbor near one of the Azores islands.

"I'm going to pay you a visit, Lars," Captain Langdon said.

"I was going to come and visit *you.*"

"Hell no, Lars. It's lunchtime and I can use a break from Navy food."

The motor launch pulled up next to the *Melody of the Seas* and deposited its passengers on the boat platform. Langdon brought one of his junior officers with him.

Captains Ragnarssen and Langdon sat down to lunch in a beautiful dining room overlooking the water. Lars invited First Officer Bob Simmons to dine with them.

"Because you're a destroyer captain," Lars said, "I'm wondering if you knew my friend Harry Fenton, the captain of the *Maltese*. He was a great guy. A lot of people are going to miss him."

"Know him?" Captain Langdon said. "Every tin can captain in the fleet knows, or knew, Harry Fenton. When God handed out brass balls, he gave Harry an extra pair. His ship was attacked by four rogue nut jobs from the Iranian Navy in small gunboats. The boats may not have been big, but they packed a wallop. Most destroyer skippers would have turned tail and outrun the bastards. Not Harry. He charged *at* them, not away from them. He blew all four out of the water, but not without taking a rocket hit to the bridge. He got a nasty chest wound and broke his nose when he was flung across the bridge. Besides a Purple Heart for his injuries, he was awarded the Navy Cross. I met him at a reunion at the Naval Academy where he gave a speech. Harry takes his job seriously but not himself. He's got the greatest self-deprecating sense of humor I've ever heard. Did I mention that I wrote a book about Harry Fenton, titled *An Ocean of Courage?* It was published a few months ago by The Naval Institute. I got in a couple of great interviews with Harry before he left the Navy and took command of that goddam *Maltese* ship."

"How's the book doing, Jim?"

"It's doing well in colleges and universities with Naval ROTC programs. The book is required reading at a lot of them. Of course, every destroyer captain in the fleet has bought a copy. It gets me sick to think that Harry may be dead."

"*May* be dead? Jim, you can't be holding out hope that somehow the people on the *Maltese* are still alive."

"Until I see proof, Lars, I'm assuming that Harry is missing in action, but not dead. Harry has a way of looking death in the mouth and punching out a few teeth. On that subject, can you guys bring me up to speed on the crazy *Maltese Incident?*"

"Crazy is the appropriate word, Jim, and it looks like the *Melody* and the *Forrest Sherman* have dipped our toes in crazy waters too."

"This is frustrating as hell," Langdon said. "First the *Maltese Incident*, and now this sea monster that's buzzing our two ships."

"The last thing I expected on a cruise was to be attacked by a whale," Lars said.

"To be accurate, captain," Simmons said, "he didn't attack us, he just bumped up against us."

"And we're not sure if the friggin thing is a whale," Langdon said. "We're calling it that because it's so huge, but two of my people and one of yours said it had the fin characteristics of a shark."

"That's my observation as well," Lars said. "It looked more like a shark—a giant shark."

"What does all this have to do with the *Maltese Incident?*" Langdon asked.

"It's completely weird, unexpected, and out of the ordinary, just like the *Maltese Incident*." Lars said. "It's strange, like a Black Swan. We have nothing to connect the two occurrences, but they do share one trait—weirdness."

CHAPTER NINE

"Hey, Pickle-puss, why so sad?" Meg asked me. "You're the most positive-thinking person I ever met, and you're standing there like a droop. How about a martini?"

We were in our stateroom for a pre-dinner cocktail.

"Yes, a martini would be great," I said. "I may be a positive thinker, but I'm also a realist. We're on a luxury cruise ship, Meg, not a military vessel. Because I'm a safety nut, this ship is outfitted for emergencies. We carry more than enough fire extinguishers, a zillion life preservers, and more lifeboats than we need. I've personally trained the crew on handling fire hoses and fire-fighting equipment. We're ready for problems—most problems. But dinosaurs are a problem I didn't anticipate, not to mention not knowing where we are."

"Harry, are you kidding? Before we left port I helped your first officer take a firearms inventory. Just look at the gun and ammunition lockers and you'd think we're preparing for war. Hell, we even stock hand grenades. And, as you said at the meeting, Bob Flowers figured out how to make gunpowder and bullets. Give me a smile—and a kiss."

"To an extent, you're right, Meg, we do pack a lot of firepower. I rigged this ship to handle an attack by a band of terrorists. But I never counted on what we're up against. First, we seem to have lost our place in time. We aren't in the same time or even the same era as when we left. Those goddam dinosaurs we saw were supposed to be extinct millions of years ago. The big problem, as I see it, is that everything eventually runs out, especially fuel. When I was in the Navy I was trained to prepare for the unexpected. But I wasn't trained for this shit."

Meg's right, as usual. She says that I'm a positive guy and I am. I'm raising all these problems because I've learned that my wife's brain is a force of nature when it comes to analyzing complicated situations. She has a habit of nailing the right solution.

"This ship will run out of fuel sooner than later, Meg. What do we do then? The simple answer is that we need to set up a compound ashore. It really isn't an option but a necessity. But how do we fit in and protect ourselves? We can't join the local Chamber of Commerce to get our bearings. We'll be in a struggle for survival. I'm sorry to be talking like this, honey, but my reality-thinking is starting to edge out my positive-thinking. So now that I've ruined our cocktail break, what are your thoughts, Meg?"

"Well, let's start with another martini and work from there."

"That's another thing, Meg. We'll run out of booze."

"Listen, Captain Handsome, let's turn the old positive-thinking Harry Fenton loose. Let's think about the good things. We have each other, and that won't run out. 'Till death do us part,' remember. As long as I'm with you, a herd of dinosaurs couldn't upset me. I have no idea about this weird time-warp thing we find ourselves in, but we've got a shipload of smart— really smart— people. We'll need to shift our thinking from analyzing and trading securities, to building a new life ashore. I'll bet a few amateur carpenters are aboard who can train the rest of us. We can build a village. When we were ashore I noticed a waterfall on that mountain near the beach. If we put our heads together I'm sure we can rig a hydroelectric pump for electricity."

"And who will be in charge of shooing away a curious *tyrannosaurus*?" I said with a smirk. My negativity act was getting its desired result. Meg's dazzling mind was in full throttle.

"Hey, Mr. Positive, if we can rig electricity, we can build an electric fence to surround Malta Town."

"Malta Town? That has a nice ring to it. But I hate the idea that we may never get back to where we came from."

"So what if we never do?" Meg said. "We get to start life all over again. We have each other, for starts. To me that's all that matters. We already know we can make extra bullets and gun powder. We can start a softball league. Hell, I bet we can even figure out a way to distill booze. The important thing is to show everyone our positivity and do everything we can to keep life alive. We can do it, Harry. But it's critical that you keep a smile on your handsome face."

"Have I told you recently how much I love you?" I said. "You're waking up the positive in me as you always do."

"So, what are you going to do about it?"

"Let's start with a kiss. We'll think of something else for after dinner."

CHAPTER TEN

"I recommend that you weigh anchor now, Captain Lars," Langdon said. "We'll be right behind you—looking out for prehistoric sharks."

Lars gave the command to his anchor room to pull up the hook as the *Melody of the Seas* sounded a blast from the ship's horn. Captain Langdon did the same on the *Forrest Sherman*. As the *Sherman's* anchor cleared the bottom, the Navy theme song, "Anchors Aweigh," carried over the waters.

"I'm envious of you, Captain Jim. I don't have such a stirring theme to play."

"Try Neil Diamond singing *Kentucky Woman*, Lars. You civilian ships need to be flexible."

Both ships began their journey to Lisbon, Portugal. They cruised a half-mile apart, the *Forrest Sherman* taking a position as combat support for the *Melody*. Captain Lars and Captain Jim posted extra lookouts and ordered their sonar screens to be monitored constantly for any appearance of the giant shark.

Captain Jim was on the bridge of the *Forrest Sherman*, sipping a cup of coffee and looking at the sonar scope. They were two hours outside of Lisbon.

"Holy shit," he yelled, "prepare for impact."

The ship hit an object, or an object hit the ship. Langdon called the gun deck and ordered the five-inch guns to prepare to fire.

"All engines ahead full, right full rudder, stand clear the depth charge racks."

The *Forrest Sherman* was equipped with a modern rack that enabled the depth charges to be rolled off by remote control, either one at a time or an entire rack of 12 MK6 depth charges. Captain Jim opted to release one at a time. Behind the ship a huge plume of seawater reached for the sky after the charge detonated.

"The target is afloat off our stern, sir," yelled the depth charge station chief into his radio. "He's in one piece. Looks like the depth charge killed him with the shock wave."

"Mark the target," Captain Langdon said.

"Aye, aye, sir." The chief fired a life preserver pole with a pennant on top directly at the floating giant. Captain Jim turned the ship in a circle, bringing it alongside the shark. Captain Lars on the *Melody* kept a distance while the *Forrest Sherman* maneuvered. Sailors from the deck crew shot lances into the carcass and a diver wrapped the dead fish with lines that were connected to stanchions aboard.

"Lieutenant, alert the port in Lisbon that our ship will be towing a huge fish," Langdon said to the officer of the deck. He then radioed Captain Lars.

"Lars, it looks like we bagged a winner. I'm slowing to ten knots while dragging the thing to Lisbon. I've alerted the port that we're towing dead marine life."

"I think I've just found my favorite fishing partner, Jim. Nice shooting."

As the *Forrest Sherman* proceeded on its course, the water around the giant shark erupted into a feeding frenzy. Every fish for miles around, including sharks, joined in the feast. As the ship cleared the breakwater heading toward Lisbon, the only part of the giant that remained was a five-foot section of vertebra. Jim called Lars on the *Melody*.

"Lars, I feel like the *Old Man and the Sea*—a big catch, but nothing to show for it."

"Don't worry, Jim, at least you deterred his amorous advances toward our ships. We have plenty of photos of our big friend before he was eaten. I think we have enough pictures and eyewitnesses to convince people that there's something weird in the waters of the Azores."

"Yeah, but I'm not sure we've seen the end of the weirdness," Captain Jim said. "Something tells me that it's just begun."

CHAPTER ELEVEN

"Good afternoon, ladies and gentlemen, Shepard Smith reporting for *Fox News*. I have nothing new to report about the disappearance of the ship *Maltese*. She's been missing for two weeks and hopes of finding survivors are growing slimmer every day. Along with her crew of 35 and 950 passengers, the *Maltese Incident* will go down as one of the greatest of maritime mysteries ever.

"But there is other shipping news to tell you about, and this story is about as strange as news gets. We have been receiving reports best described as weird. The Norwegian Cruise Line ship, the *Melody of the Seas*, has apparently encountered a shark on steroids. The ship is currently tied to a dock in Lisbon, Portugal. Aldo Costa, a reporter with our *Fox News* affiliate in Lisbon is on the bridge of the *Melody of the Seas* speaking to Captain Lars Ragnarssen, who will tell us about the sighting of a truly giant shark."

"Hello, Shepard, Aldo Costa here for *Fox News*. This is one of the strangest stories I've ever filed. As you said, I'm here with the captain of the *Melody of the Seas*, Lars Ragnarssen."

"Hi, Aldo, welcome aboard the *Melody of the Seas*," Captain Ragnarssen said, "and hello to the viewers of *Fox News*. Yes, the stories you've heard are true but very strange. Besides myself, many of our crew and passengers have reported a gigantic shark swimming near the ship. The size estimates are anywhere from 60 to 100 feet. At one point the fish breached, completely leaving the water. Our quick-thinking lookout managed to get a photograph. Here it is."

Costa held the photograph up for the camera.

"I'll email this to you, Shepard. It's amazing—a fish bigger than a whale."

"Captain Ragnarssen, I understand that an American warship, a destroyer, was cruising nearby your ship."

"Yes, Aldo," Lars said, "The captain of the *USS Forrest Sherman* was kind enough to volunteer his ship as our escort. When the monster fish appeared while we steamed toward Lisbon, Captain Langdon dropped a depth charge on the animal, killing it. He tried to tow its remains to port, about two hours away from our position, but the carcass was attacked and eaten by hundreds of fish. Only a small part of the skeleton remained, but we have photographs of the fish taken by passengers and crew."

"Have you spotted any other of these big sharks, captain?" Smith asked.

"A few of our passengers reported seeing a huge dorsal fin off our stern, and one near the bow."

"And here it is, ladies and gentlemen," Smith said, as the camera zoomed on the photo of the shark leaping out of the water. "Joining us on the line is Professor Max Feigenbaum, a paleontologist from the American Museum of Natural History here in Manhattan. Dr. Feigenbaum, what do you make of this photograph and the others I've shown you?"

"I'm astonished," Feigenbaum said, "simply astonished. Assuming that these photos are authentic, and I don't believe that the people on the ship would lie, we're looking at an amazing breakthrough in paleontology. In 1938 a *Coelacanth*, a fish assumed to be long extinct, was found in the West Indian Ocean. But this discovery far exceeds that one. And the fact that the captain reported multiple sightings only adds to the shock."

"Dr. Feigenbaum," Smith said, "what kind of fish are we looking at in the photos?"

"It's a *Megalodon*, a giant shark that we thought became extinct millions of years ago. Shepard, this is the greatest development in paleontology since the discovery of the first dinosaur fossil. I don't have to worry where my research will be directed in the future."

"Thank you Dr. Feigenbaum. I'm sure we'll be talking from time to time."

"So, there you have it, ladies and gentlemen. Two unexplained sea stories—a vanishing ship and prehistoric shark sightings. As Dr. Feigenbaum told us, live fossils from the time of the dinosaurs are swimming in the ocean near Portugal.

"And let's not forget the *Maltese Incident*. Along with a crew of 35 and 950 passengers, the ship is still missing—two weeks and counting."

CHAPTER TWELVE

Our regular monthly meeting was scheduled for after lunch. Meg asked me if she could conduct the meeting and make a special announcement. Meg loves to hit me with surprises. The meeting would be relatively short, because the major plans that Meg, Randy, and I were working on needed more detail before we could make them an agenda item.

After Meg welcomed everyone, she unfurled her surprise.

"I was helping our ship's librarian straighten out the shelves the other day, when I came across a book hidden behind a stack of other books."

She held up a book with its cover obscured from me because of the angle of where I sat.

"Before I tell you about the book, I first want to tell you that I've come up with a new name for my husband."

Uh oh, I thought. Here comes the surprise.

"Harry's new name is 'Captain Humility.' Here's why, and here's why you should all read this book. Unfortunately, our library has only one copy, which was hidden until now."

She held up the book again.

"*An Ocean of Courage – The Story of Captain Harry Fenton* by Captain James Langdon, United States Navy."

Meg then blew her nose and wiped away a tear.

"I knew about Harry's reputation as a war hero, but I didn't know the depth of his courage until I read this book. Harry received the Navy Cross for leading his destroyer into combat in the Persian Gulf when it was attacked by four rogue Iranian gunboats. Rather than outrun the boats, Harry charged his destroyer at them, sinking all four. He was almost killed when an enemy rocket exploded on the bridge, earning him the Purple Heart for his injuries as well as the Navy Cross for valor. I had no idea of the history of the Navy Cross. I just learned that it's the highest decoration a Navy person can earn, just below the Medal of Honor."

As Meg intended, the audience went ape shit, screaming and applauding. Now it was my turn to wipe away some tears. I was the one who hid the book behind the others in the library. Maybe my mother's words took root. "True courage is doing the right thing when nobody else is looking," she often said. Okay, I served my country and took some risks doing so. I really didn't want my Navy exploits to define who I am. But Meg thought my experiences should be publicized. After she sat down next to me, Randy got up to say a few words. I leaned over and whispered into Meg's ear.

"You said you had a surprise, and you obviously did."

She turned her head and kissed me.

"So now I know how you got that broken nose," she said.

I had told her that I was punched by a jealous husband.

Chef Carlos walked down the center aisle carrying a huge cake, made with some of our remaining baking goods. He inscribed it with red, white and blue lettering: "*An Ocean of Courage—The Story of Captain Harry Fenton.*"

The meeting completely fell apart, especially when Randy announced drinks on the house. A few people started chanting, "Speech, speech, speech," and it caught on with the entire crowd. I've never been shy about speaking in public, but under the circumstances I felt like this was my first time.

"I'll admit that I'm the one who hid the book behind the stacks," I said. "My service to the country that I love, although I'm proud of it, is part of a past life. I now have a life with a wonderful woman, a great group of people, and a new home in God knows wherever we are. I don't know about Meg's idea of calling me Captain Humility, but I guess it beats what she often calls me—Captain Asshole."

CHAPTER THIRTEEN

"Federal Bureau of Investigation, Director Watson's office, may I help you?"

"This is Bill Carlini at CIA. Put Sarah on please."

"Hi, Bill, how's my favorite spy?"

"Well, Sarah, I may soon become your favorite unemployed spy."

"What are you talking about? You're the best director the CIA ever had, at least since I've been around. Something tells me you're getting heat from somewhere, and my guess is that it's coming from 1600 Pennsylvania Avenue."

"You're perceptive as always, Sarah. Hey, you know I don't like talking on the phone, and I don't care how secure the damn thing is. I'd like to see you in your office in a half hour. I'll have someone with me."

"Who'll be with you? Let me guess—Buster?"

"How did you know that?"

"Bill, I've known you for a long time. Anytime you're upset about something you call on super spook Buster. Can you give me a hint at what we'll talk about?"

"I'll bet you know that too, Sarah. Take a guess."

"*The Maltese Incident*? How's my guessing score?"

"One hundred percent as usual, my friend. Buster and I will be there in a half hour."

***

I've been known as Buster for as long as I can remember. I'm a Coptic Christian, and my given name is Gamal Akhbar. My name and my Middle Eastern appearance that I got from my Egyptian parents, usually prompts smartass questions like, "Where did you park your camel?" Besides Buster and Gamal Akhbar, my other name is Charles Atkins. Spies can't have enough different identities. I also speak fluent Arabic. I guess you could call me a jihadi's worst nightmare—I look like them, I sound like them, but I'm not one of them. I hunt them down and kill them. Bill Carlini, my boss and friend, has something sensitive for me to handle, like he always does. Add Sarah Watson to the brew and I can tell it's something big.

"Great to see you two again," Sarah Watson said. "Bill, I'm glad you brought Buster along."

Like I said, something big was coming.

"Bill, you're not the only one who's been getting heat from the White House about the *Maltese Incident,*" Watson said. "They've been all over me too. The president wants a joint operation of the CIA and FBI. It isn't every day that an American cruise ship in international waters suddenly vanishes. A witness on a nearby yacht recalled seeing the *Maltese* bathed in light and then disappear. We haven't been able to contact the captain of the yacht but we're still working on it. Buster, Bill Carlini and I want you to take over as the lead agent on the case. Besides the fact that over a thousand people disappeared, the White House is all over the map on this incident because of the captain of the *Maltese,* Harry Fenton. The guy mustered out of the Navy last year with the rank of full captain even though he was only 40 years old. In a brief time he became a legend among destroyer captains with his heroic actions in the Gulf. The Navy Department, backed by the White House, had plans for Fenton to become an admiral. After he left the Navy he was asked to speak to school groups to recruit kids to apply to the Naval Academy. The president himself once met Fenton and apparently took a big liking to him. Your thoughts, Buster?"

"I've read everything there is to read about this case, and I admit that I'm stumped. From what we know, it doesn't look like the ship sank—it just disappeared into thin air."

"That's why we want a super spook on the case, my friend," said Carlini.

"I'm not sure where to start. Any suggestions?"

"Yes," Sarah said, butting in, "I do have a suggestion, and I think you'll like it. We're booking you on a cruise on the *Melody of the Seas*, a Norwegian Line cruise ship that left New York two days ago. She's headed toward Lisbon, Portugal and will cruise through the Azores, the part of the ocean where the *Maltese* went missing. You'll fly to Lisbon and board the ship there. If we ever break this case it will be the result of basic cop work, talking to people, asking questions, and taking notes, all of which you're great at. Our entire government is up to its eyeballs in theories about the *Maltese Incident*. The bottom line is that a ship disappeared, not sank—disappeared."

Great, I thought. They want me to investigate a case that's almost impossible to investigate.

"Enjoy your cruise, Buster," said Carlini. "Please come back with some facts—no more theories. We need some answers. Hell, the ship's been missing for three weeks."

CHAPTER FOURTEEN

"How long have we been gone? I've lost track." Randy said. Meg, Randy, and I stood on the outer portion of the bridge. We were about to begin a planning meeting, so we figured we'd start with some fresh air.

"We'll have been gone a year and a half next week," Meg said. "I don't know about you guys, but I'm starting to feel like I've been on this ship all my life."

"A year and a half?" Randy said. "The people back home must definitely think we're all dead."

"Before we get down to details, we need to talk to somebody," I said. "Dr. Rosario asked if she could talk to us. She should be here momentarily."

We heard a gentle knock on the door. Besides being an excellent physician, Theresa is extremely polite. She was invited to this meeting, so she could have just walked in, but she chose to knock.

"Hi Theresa," we all said.

"Theresa asked if she could come by and take our vitals," I said.

"That's close to the truth, Harry, because what I need to talk to you guys about is vital," Dr. Theresa said. "To put it bluntly, I'm worried about running out of medicine, especially antibiotics. I'm amazed that our supplies have lasted this long. I've been stretching them as far as I can. If somebody comes to me with a mild fever, I put him in quarantine and prescribe liquids and bed rest. I know you folks are discussing plans to move ashore. We don't know what kinds of nasty microbes we may encounter. I can't guarantee that I have enough medicine to handle every illness."

"What about huddling with Bob Flowers?" Meg suggested. "He's a damn good scientist. Hell, he figured out how we can make extra bullets and gun powder, not to mention how to distill booze. Maybe he can figure out how to stretch our medical supplies further."

"I've already met with Bob, and he definitely has some ideas," Theresa said. "We've laid out a plan for trying to replicate the most basic medicines, and once we go ashore, we're going to hunt for some natural substances. We especially need antibiotics and aspirin. Hopefully, between Bob and me, we can come up with a manufacturing process. I just wanted to alert you guys to a big problem facing us soon. A flu epidemic, God forbid, could wipe out a significant part of our little population."

"Do we know of any other people aboard who can help Theresa and Bob Flowers?" I asked.

"Yes," Randy said. "Tim Green from the research department has a biology background. He used to help us analyze potential investments in pharmaceutical companies. Harry, I think you should assign him immediately to work with Theresa and Bob."

"Oh, yeah, there's that guy Jason Thomas," Theresa said. "He's constantly asking me if he can help. He's got no medical or scientific background at all, so I keep turning him down."

"Maybe he just wants to learn, Theresa," Meg said.

"I hate to say this about anybody, but the guy gives me the creeps," Dr. Theresa said. "There's something about him that I just don't trust."

"Theresa," I said. "Thank you for sounding the alarm. This project is now a high priority item. Please keep us up to date on your progress."

***

"Dr. Theresa has put an exclamation point on this meeting." I said. "We have some big decisions to make, and we need to think about the obvious. We may be stuck in this time for the rest of our lives, and I'm not being dramatic."

Randy and Meg looked at me.

"We have no book to follow with this crazy shit, and we've got to consider the possibility that this is our fate. And if that's so, we need to think about an alternative to living on the *Maltese*. We still don't know how the hell we got here, but we need to deal with life as it's handed to us, dinosaurs and all. So, here's my opinion—we need to build a permanent home ashore."

"Thank God Ted Morton, the former owner of this ship, was a builder," Randy said. "He was an eccentric billionaire and a talented wood-working artist. Despite his vast wealth, he intended to build his own mansion with a few outbuildings on an island he owned in the Bahamas. He carried enough tools and materials on this ship to build a small city. A shame he died before he could carry out his plans."

"But like you said, Randy," I said, "Morton left a ton of building supplies in the hold of the *Maltese*, enough for us to construct a compound ashore. We've been talking about this idea for months, and now's the time to act. We kicked the can down the road, avoiding making a tough decision. We've treated this like a bad dream that would just go away. Our shore excursion crews have been bringing us a steady supply almost edible small game as well as vegetables and fruit. The future, whatever the hell that is, lies ashore, not on this rusting ship. If we wait much longer it will turn into an emergency, which will be too late. Our electricity generation is at a low ebb, and that's the most critical of our onboard systems. We've got to start planning and building now. With the professional tool shop and supplies that Morton left, we can make it happen. Let's put our heads together and assemble a committee of people who are talented with physical stuff like building and farming. Meg has some great ideas, as usual, but we need to start nailing those ideas down. God knows we have a lot of smart people aboard, and it's time to kick those brains into action. The bottom line—It's time to plan for life ashore. Your comments?"

"Electricity," Meg said. "I talked to George Donaldson, who was an electrical engineer before he joined Malta, and he's still up to speed on engineering matters. I talked to him about that waterfall on the mountain near the shoreline and my idea of hydroelectric power. He agrees with me that we can build a generating plant using materials that we have onboard. We have spare transformers on the *Maltese*, so we can capture usable electricity, not just raw juice. Donaldson thinks that we can be up and running with newly generated electricity within two months, maybe three."

"We need an electrical fence around the compound to protect us from neighboring dinosaurs," Randy said. "I think the next item on our agenda should be the physical plant of Malta Town, the structures for housing and support. Wally Bellino is the perfect guy to head that up. He was a successful real estate developer before he joined Malta, and he knows construction inside and out. I showed him the building materials stored in our hold, and he said he could build a housing compound with what's already onboard plus additional lumber from ashore."

"What about the actual construction?" I pointed out. "We need some muscle for banging nails, digging trenches, and all that kind of physical stuff. I'm thinking about the crew in the engine room, but there are only six of them. Add the deck crew of eight and we're up to fourteen. We'll need some volunteers from the rest of the people to help out, and build some muscle of their own in the process."

"I've been thinking about how many residential units we'll need," Meg said. "Of the 1,010 people aboard, 30 percent of them are married couples, which equates to 303 multi-room units and 410 single apartments. I'm sure that other people will become couples, like Harry and me. We don't have the luxury of building a suburban community of single family homes, so we'll be looking at a prehistoric version of high density housing."

"Let's not forget a hospital," Randy said. "After what Dr. Theresa pointed out, we need to think about health, especially if we're low on medicine."

"What about that guy Jason Thomas?" I said. "On the ship he always insisted that he have his own space, no matter how small."

"Some people relish their privacy," Meg said. "But Dr. Theresa doesn't trust him and refuses to work with him. Theresa's a warm, easy-going person with a keen sense about people. If she doesn't trust the guy, I'm not sure we should either."

"The guy really *is* kind of strange," I said. "I once walked into his stateroom, mistaking it for a different place. He had just laid down what looked like a prayer rug. None of my business, but he seemed nervous and made up a story that he liked having a carpet in his room. I asked him if he was a Muslim, just to be friendly. He denied it like crazy."

"Now that you mentioned it," Meg said, "he once approached me and suggested that all the women wear headscarves to cover their hair. I paid no attention to it and just forgot about the incident."

"Let's stop talking about that jerk," I said. "We have a zillion details to cover, so we'll take it one thing at a time. Management, for now, will consist of the three of us plus people that we'll add from time to time."

"This can work," Meg said. "In a short time, those dinosaurs are going to have some incredible new neighbors."

"Did you say edible new neighbors?" I asked.

CHAPTER FIFTEEN

"Buster, it's time for us to brainstorm," Bill Carlini said.

One of the things I like about Bill is that he's an obsessive compulsive, like me. Just the other day he wished me well on my cruise, and now he wants to have a brainstorming meeting before I board the ship. That was perfectly fine with me. There's nobody I enjoy brainstorming with more than Bill Carlini, and if there was ever a case that needed brainwork it was the *Maltese Incident*.

"Let's lay one theory of the *Maltese Incident* to rest," Bill said. "Any of us who heard that a ship was missing, and then heard that gigantic sea creatures swam in the same waters where the ship disappeared, and then heard that the big fish intentionally bumped against a cruise ship and a warship—well, that all screams for a conclusion—that Mr. Megashark sank the ship. What's wrong with that theory?"

"The physical evidence, or lack thereof, is what's wrong with it." I said. "We know the approximate location of the *Maltese* before it disappeared. The American government has launched a fleet of mini-subs, both manned and unmanned. I believe the number was 75 submersibles. The Navy and Coast Guard have dropped hundreds of sonar listening devices—no result. So, we need to lay that theory to rest—the theory that the fish sank the *Maltese*. With all the thwarted engineering theories I just mentioned, we should also question whether the ship sank at all. But if it didn't sink, where the hell did it go?"

"We just came to the point that makes my head spin," Carlini said. "From everything we know, the *Maltese* didn't sink, it just disappeared. But things don't just disappear, do they? And giant prehistoric sharks don't just show up, do they? We're trying like hell to connect those two dots, but the dots almost seem to repel one another."

"I think we're stuck with basic flat-foot cop work, Bill," I said. "I'd like to say that most of the cases I've crack were because of my brilliance as a CIA agent, but most of them were solved because some cop or new agent uncovered a clue that we all missed. So, I'm going to pose a theory that neither of us will like, but which makes sense because of the lack of physical evidence. And here's my theory—Mr. Megashark did *not* sink the *Maltese*."

"I think you're right, Buster. Even if there was a connection between the loss of the *Maltese* and the sightings of those giant sharks, that doesn't mean that one of the big sharks sank the ship. There may be a connection between the two events only because they're both out of the ordinary. I don't believe in coincidences. Am I thinking inside or outside of the box, Buster?"

"A bit of both, Bill. We know that the *Maltese* disappeared, and we know where it was when it happened because we have a good navigational fix. The problem is that no debris or metallic objects were found anywhere near that position. I'm going to go out on a limb and say that I'm sure that none of the sharks ate the fucking ship."

"We can agree on that, Buster. The sharks didn't eat the ship, nor did they sink it. So, we're still at the starting block. We've ruled out an explosion because there was no debris. We've also ruled out the possibility that the ship suddenly sank, again because of no debris. I started out by saying that the *Maltese Incident* and the shark sightings had some connection, but we have no idea what."

"We can also eliminate another possibility," I said. "We know that the shark or sharks tend to bump into ships, just like they did to the *Melody*. It's theoretically possible that the fish loosened some plates and let in enough water to sink the ship. But we've already concluded that the *Maltese* did not sink, no matter what the cause. I can use a drink."

"Since when do you drink on the job, Mr. Super Spook?" Bill said.

"I'm about to begin my assignment on a cruise ship and I've never encountered a case like this before. I'm going to be spending a lot of time chatting with people at the ship's bar? How about joining me for a drink in the CIA lounge after our meeting."

"Buster, your father was a cop. Both of my parents were cops. We grew up with cop talk. There's one thing I always heard my parents say about a tough case. The solution is seldom the result of brilliance on the part of a detective. You said the same thing. The solution is usually the result of basic police work—pounding the pavement and talking to people. The more you talk to people, the more people talk to you, and all of a sudden, a clue pops up in the middle of a conversation. I think it's accurate to say that right now we're clueless."

"Bill, you're right, I need to interview people—but who? We've already spoken to a lot of cruise ship officers. So, who the hell do I talk to now?"

"Max Feigenbaum, Buster. He's the guy who was on *Fox News* the other day. Remember, he's a paleontologist from the American Museum of Natural History. He told the anchorman Shepard Smith, that he was going to Lisbon to set up shop and track down information about the giant sharks. You know Smith personally. Why don't you call him and ask where in Lisbon the professor is."

"News media people hate to share leads, Bill. I'll hold Shepard in the background and call him only if I need to. But how about this? I'll adopt one of my alter egos that I've used before. I'll become a reporter for *The Investigator,* the new (make-believe) magazine. People love to talk to reporters, and they expect to be asked a lot of questions. I'll simply call the American Museum of Natural History and ask where Feigenbaum is."

"Good thinking, Buster. I'll take you up on that drink now."

CHAPTER SIXTEEN

"Meg, may I have a word with you?" Randy Borg said as we encountered each other on the promenade deck.

I could tell that Randy had something important to talk about. He always begins heavy conversations with, "May I have a word with you?"

"Sure Randy, what's up?"

"You and Harry getting married has been the greatest thing to hit this God-forsaken ship. Everybody can tell that you two are very much in love. When you told us all about that book about Harry, I thought people were going to carry you both around on their shoulders."

"Well, I'll admit that I'm in love with Harry," Meg said.

"A few of us were having drinks the other night," Randy said. "Somebody suggested that you and Harry are like the president and first lady of the *Maltese*. I agree with that. You two bring a sense of, I don't know, a sense of continuity to this crazy situation. If it weren't for you two, our weird situation would be a lot worse."

Randy's a great guy, but sometimes he takes forever to make a point. Where the hell is he going with this? I figured I'd ask.

"Randy, thanks for your kind comments, but let me ask you—are you writing a song and looking for lyrics?"

Randy cracked up.

"You and Harry have the greatest wiseass senses of humor on the ship."

"So, two dinosaurs walk into a bar," I said.

When he stopped laughing, Randy got serious.

"At the beginning of this conversation I said I'd like to have a word with you, and I'm afraid that I'm not being too clear. I'm the CEO of the company, and this ship is our property. Some people call me boss, but that's inaccurate. I may be the CEO, but I'm not the boss. Harry is, and you help make him the boss."

"Harry *is* a natural leader, Randy. Putting him in operational charge was a great idea. So, what's on your mind?"

"I want Harry to be *elected* as our leader. It would give him a greater position at the top. It would also give the passengers and crew a vested interest in his success and the success of everyone on the *Maltese*. God knows what we're facing, but having Harry Fenton as our leader, not just titular but elected, will make our crazy situation a lot more palatable. We know that we'll be setting up a community compound ashore. It's in our American blood to do things democratically, and to pull that off we need elected leadership. And he's got a great first lady to back him up. I'd be happy to be his campaign manager."

"Do you expect opposition?"

"Not at all. Well, there's that crazy kid in the boiler room. But no, I want to give people more of a direct connection to Harry. My only concern is that he won't go for it. He has a sense of modesty that's inspiring. Hell, he even hid that book about him in the library. You jokingly referred to him as 'Captain Humility' and it isn't just funny, it's the truth. He takes his job seriously, but not himself. I want you to break it to him, and, if necessary, talk him into it. Meg, I'm overstating the obvious when I say that you have an enormous amount of influence on the captain."

"We're not going to call him Mr. President are we?" I asked. "He won't go for that."

"No, Meg. Harry is the captain. We'll just make it an official vote by the crew and passengers rather than his simply being one of my appointments.

"I think this is a good idea, Randy. If he lets it go to his head, I'm just the one to slap him around. Right now, he's on watch—he insists on standing watch just like a subordinate. I'll go to see him now."

I really did like Randy's idea. We're talking about moving ashore and creating a town. Soon we'll no longer be the crew and passengers of the *Maltese*, but citizens of Malta Town. If Harry's going to govern, he'll need the consent of the governed. In a most simplistic way, that's what democracy is all about. Unless Harry is elected, he will be a dictator, something that he'd hate. I just hope he goes for Randy's idea. Maybe we'll call him Mr. Mayor. Everybody loves Harry, and nobody as much as me. People will love and respect him even more if they vote to put him in office. Randy didn't get to be CEO without having good ideas.

CHAPTER SEVENTEEN

Steve Michaels and his wife Grace recently took possession of Steve's retirement toy, a brand new 43-foot Grand Banks trawler. He loved the water all his life, and he always looked at the Grand Banks as the pinnacle of boating, even though its speed topped out at only 20 knots. With a sticker price of over $1 million, he saw the boat as a fitting cap to his career as an executive at Microsoft. They bought the boat from a dealer in Lisbon, where they vacationed at the home of friends, the Dixons.

Phil and Arlene Dixon accompanied them on their boat's first trip. The Michaels named the boat *Terabyte*, to celebrate Steve's successful digital career. Steve plotted a course for Sao Miguel, one of the islands in the Azores, where they would visit with other friends. Their 900-mile journey would take almost two days from Lisbon, depending on the speed they could maintain.

Steve Michaels and Phil Dixon were avid fishermen all their lives. But when he thought about fish guts all over his new yacht, Steve was careful to cover the rear deck with paper and canvas.

"Don't go catching any sharks you guys," Grace said. "They're too big and messy for our beautiful new boat."

"Don't worry, hon, we're after game fish. Make sure you keep the camera handy."

Shortly after they entered the Azores, Phil Dixon felt a heavy tug on his rod.

"I think I've got something big, Steve."

Twenty-five feet behind the boat a beautiful blue marlin cleared the water. Steve checked the straps on Phil's fishing chair.

"You're going to be busy right through cocktail hour, Phil."

The marlin cleared the water again. Then came another, and another, and another. Soon the water behind the boat erupted into a riotous scene of jumping blue marlins and other game fish.

"Get the camera, hon," Steve said to Grace. "I've never seen anything like this before."

Grace walked up to the rail with her camera, taking pictures as she did.

"Something down there is scaring the hell out of those fish, guys," Grace said. "Remember, no shark fishing. Holy shit, what was that?"

The boat had just taken a 45-degree list to port. As the only one strapped down, Phil didn't move. Steve, Grace, and Arlene tumbled across the deck and crashed against the portside bulkhead. When the boat finally righted itself, Phil unbuckled himself and first went to Grace, who sprained her wrist from slamming against the bulkhead. He then checked on Arlene, who seemed to have a fractured ankle. Steve's forehead was bleeding but not too badly.

"Was that a goddam whale?" Grace yelled. She had no sooner uttered the words when they felt a powerful slamming motion against the hull. The boat listed, this time to starboard, not as severely as the first time.

"Dear God," Phil said, as he grasped the railing and looked outward. A dorsal fin, which looked like it was at least 10 feet in height, cruised by them.

"What the hell is that thing?" Steve asked.

"Whatever it is it keeps coming closer. It's like he's circling us for another hit."

"Mayday, mayday, mayday," Steve yelled into his radio, using the international code word for an emergency.

"This is *Terabyte*, a 43-foot Grand Banks trawler that has just been attacked by an extremely large shark." He then gave the coordinates of the boat's position.

"I read you, *Terabyte*," came a reply, in perfect English, thank God. The man spoke with a slightly Southern accent. "This is *Glory Jane*, Captain Mickey Smith speaking. Just leave the big fella alone, captain, and he'll ignore you. How large is the shark? Over."

"This is *Terabyte*. Four people aboard estimate that the animal is at least 60 feet long, possibly longer, over." Captain Mickey looked at his friend Adalberto and they both laughed.

"*Terabyte*, this is *Glory Jane*. A bit early for cocktails, I think. I repeat, just leave the fish alone and he'll let you be, over."

"*Glory Jane*, this is *Terabyte*. You don't underst…," Steve said.

The *Glory Jane* skipper heard a brief noise that sounded like a shout.

"*Terabyte* this is *Glory Jane*. You cut out on me, buddy. Everything okay? I say again, is everything okay? *Terabyte*, *Terabyte*, this is *Glory Jane*. Come in please."

***

The Portuguese Coast Guard filed a report with the United States Coast Guard because *Terabyte* was registered in the U.S. A search boat found the 43-foot Grand Banks in 200 feet of water. Something large had penetrated its hull, leaving a gaping hole. Divers found strange teeth marks all over her hull, as well as a tooth that measured a foot long. They also found the partial remains of two human beings near the boat.

CHAPTER EIGHTEEN

"Whoever heard of electing a captain?" I said. "Captains are appointed."

"Not quite, Mr. Furrowed Brow," Meg said. "Randy didn't pick you all on his own. You were installed as captain by a vote of the Malta Investments board. Randy just delivered the message. On big cruise ships, the same thing goes. No single individual appoints a captain. They're elected by a group, a board."

"Okay, Ms. Picky One. More than one person gets to select a captain, unless it's a small boat or it's owned by an individual. Can you imagine a large group of people responding to an election call for a ship's captain? 'All in favor, say aye.' I don't think so. What the hell does the average person know about running a ship?"

"Hey, Mr. Knucklehead, open your mind. Randy didn't say that he needs help in picking leadership. Hell, he's an accomplished senior executive. But given our weird circumstance, Randy wants you to be formally established as our leader by the people aboard the *Maltese*. Your title will still be captain, but you'll be more like a mayor."

"Will that mean that people can't call me Knucklehead?"

"I called you *Mister* Knucklehead. See how much I respect you?"

"After I got out of the Navy, a group of politicos wanted me to run for Governor of New York. I thought about it for a while but took a pass. What you're suggesting is different—a popular election of a man who holds a technical leadership job. Besides, for an election to mean anything, it's got to be possible for somebody else to run. Do you have anyone else in mind who could take my job?"

Meg moved closer to me and wrapped her arms around my waist. Damn, this woman knows how to get my attention.

"That's the point, Harry. Randy wants you to be acknowledged as our leader. Again, I remind you of our bizarre circumstances. He wants people to have a stake in the ship. God knows, unless we can find a way back to where we came from, our lives will hit the reset button. Eventually, as we've discussed, we'll move to land. We'll need some form of governance—with a strong, thoughtful leader in charge—a hero like you."

Meg walked over to the coffee station and poured a couple of mugs. I could tell she was giving me time to think.

"Democracy is a great thing, Meg, but it depends on the kind of group. No military organization, for example, is run like a democracy. It's like, 'here's your leader, salute him.' And the same goes for private business. With Malta Investments, sure there's a board, but Randy makes all sorts of unilateral decisions. And he was picked by the board, not by popular vote of the company's employees."

Meg looked down at the deck. She was obviously planning her next debate point.

"So how about a proclamation, Harry?" Meg said, with her talented voice of compromise.

"Maybe at one of our general meetings Randy will ask for a 'vote of confidence' for our captain. I don't know if you're aware how much people love and respect you. You know how much I love you because I tell you all the time. With the people aboard, you're one popular guy, especially after I told them about the book that discusses your heroism in the Gulf. And by the way, I'm sure you've noticed that the people on this ship are smart. They know a good leader when they see one, and they definitely have one in you. So, how's that for a compromise? Randy will propose a proclamation of appreciation for Harry, our fearless leader. Now I've got to convince Randy that we should go for a proclamation rather than a vote. But looking down the road, we'll need some sort of elected government after we move ashore. You know, consent of the governed and all that. I think you will make a perfect mayor."

I could see where Randy and Meg are going with this. They're trying to make the best decision for the entire ship. I should have been flattered, but I just felt plain awkward.

"Did Randy put you up to this?"

"Of course. Randy knows how much I love you, and he figured I should open the subject. So is it a deal?"

"Deal. Do you promise not to call me Knucklehead?"

"You have my solemn promise, Dickbrain."

CHAPTER NINETEEN

I almost signed the passenger manifest as "Buster" when I boarded the *Melody of the Seas* last week. Instead, I signed as George Atkins, one of my aliases. The ship is still docked in Lisbon and I sat in a café going through news clippings. It's amazing how many clues come from newspaper articles, a lesson I'd learned over the years. A good thing Lisbon is a cosmopolitan city with English language translations in most of the big papers. I paged through the *International New York Times,* formerly known as the *International Edition of the New York Times,* preceded by the *International Herald Tribune.* It's always my favorite when I travel. Thank God, the owner of the magazine café is a pack rat and I have over six months of back issues to peruse. "Holy shit," I said out loud, which I followed with an apology to an elderly couple sitting near me. An article had just caught my attention.

"A Series of Strange Ocean Incident Startles Authorities"

The New York Times

by Jonathan Golding

"Portuguese authorities in Lisbon just announced that a 43-foot pleasure yacht was attacked by unidentified marine life and sank. The boat, a luxury trawler manufactured by Grand Banks, was found on the seabed in 200 feet of water off the coast of Portugal in the Azores. The partial remains of two human beings were found near the boat's wreckage. The vessel had a large hole in its hull and strange teeth marks were found all over the boat. One tooth was recovered, measuring a foot in length. It appears to be a shark's tooth, but according to a paleontologist from the American Museum of Natural History, its size suggests that it belonged to a *Megalodon,* a prehistoric shark that grew to over 60 feet in length. The paleontologist, Dr. Max Feigenbaum, told the *Times* that he had investigated other reports of giant sharks, all of which occurred in the Azores off Portugal. According to eyewitnesses, a huge beast rammed a cruise ship and an American destroyer, but it did no damage. A photograph showing the giant shark leaping out of water was taken by a lookout on the *Melody of the Seas*, a cruise ship. According to Feigenbaum, scientists thought the *Megalodon* had been extinct for millions of years. He called the sightings, 'A historical breakthrough in paleontology.' Dr. Feigenbaum has set up a research office in Lisbon, Portugal."

It's time to talk to this guy, I thought. I looked in my notes on my cellphone. The address of Feigenbaum's temporary office was a couple of blocks from the café. I still had no idea what a giant shark, prehistoric or not, could have to do with the disappearance of the *Maltese*, but it's my job to think of myself as a flat-foot investigator. I never saw a clue look me in the eye and say, "Hi, I'm your clue."

So, I put on my bullshit detecting cap and walked toward Feigenbaum's office. I had befriended the owner of the café and he let me put my stack of newspapers in a back room. From my previous dealings with scientists, I know that there's one thing they like as much as grant money, and that's publicity. When I tell him I'm a magazine reporter, he won't shut up.

***

"Good morning. I'm Philip Thompson," I said, using yet another of my aliases. "I'm a reporter with *The Investigator,* a new magazine that examines strange subjects. I'd like to speak to Dr. Feigenbaum."

As I expected, Feigenbaum swung open the door and almost sprinted across the room to shake my hand. He escorted me into the main research office to show me his team at work.

"Welcome to the *Megalodon* research team, Mr. Thompson," said Feigenbaum, grinning like a kid at Christmas. He turned to the people in his office. "Everybody, this gentleman is a reporter for a new magazine called *The Investigator.* He's researching the *Megalodon* sightings. Mr. Thompson, I'm not sure we can answer all of your questions, but we'll try."

I started asking questions of the six people in the room. I could tell that Dr. Feigenbaum was enjoying every minute of it.

"We even employ a young man, Peter Franklin, who's a photographic expert," Feigenbaum said. "He verified that every photo of the shark is authentic."

Franklin looked at me as if he knew me. I then recalled that I once used Franklin on a terrorism investigation to verify photos.

"What did you say your name was?" Franklin asked.

"Thompson, that's Philip Thompson."

The guy looked confused, as if he didn't really buy my identification.

"Hey, Max," a young American woman said to Feigenbaum, "maybe we should refer Mr. Thompson to that nut case who keeps telling people that he saw a ship disappear."

Max furrowed his brow. He didn't want to lose his new publicity source.

"What nut case?" I blurted. "Did you say he claims he saw a ship disappear?"

"Angela," said Feigenbaum. "That man is quite insane. Let's not waste our guest's time with him."

"That's okay, Dr. Feigenbaum," I said. "I often get great quotes from crazy people. Where can I find this guy?"

"He works at Silva's Boatyard just two blocks from here," Angela said. "His name is Alfonso Avila. He has partially gray hair, speaks perfect English, and is really a nice guy, if a bit nuts. He lived in the States for most of his life. After his parents died, he decided to move back to his native Portugal. I guess he's somewhere in his late 40s."

***

After my meeting with the *Megalodon* team, I walked to Silva's Boatyard a few blocks away. The yard was large, about two acres, and housed some of the most beautiful yachts I'd ever seen. This is no small-time operator, I thought. I asked for Alfonso Avila and was directed to a man who was just about to leave the yard. I identified myself (my fake self) and invited him to lunch. He agreed, without enthusiasm.

"Sure," Avila said, "I'll have lunch with you, but I warn you, journalists are not my favorite people. I'll explain later." He told me to call him Al.

After we finished lunch, I gently asked Al about his claim of having seen a ship disappear.

"Al, I've heard that you witnessed something strange about a ship steaming in the Azores. Do you care to comment for *The Investigator*?"

"Why not? You'll learn why they call me Crazy Al."

"Your English is perfect, Al, I don't mind saying. If I detect any accent at all, it sounds like Brooklyn. You make my job as an American reporter a lot easier."

"Well, I lived in the States for 40 of my 49 years, and I'm still an American citizen. I grew up in Brooklyn and graduated from Brooklyn Tech. By the way, my friend, you can cut the bullshit about being a magazine reporter. You're either CIA or FBI or both."

"How did you know that? Not that I'm admitting it."

"I spent 20 years with the American ONI, the Office of Naval Intelligence. That's where I get my pension income. I retired with the Navy rank of commander. So, I'm a detective like you, which is why I can spot you a mile away. Also, as we were waiting for our food to be served, I Googled *The Investigator* on my cellphone. It doesn't exist, which is fine by me. I feel more comfortable talking to spies than the press. You're much more honest than reporters. You can ask me anything you want. Crazy Al is at your service."

"Please call me Buster. Al, you embarrass me, or maybe I've embarrassed myself. As you know from your experience I can't go into much detail about myself. Yes, I am a CIA agent, *not* a magazine reporter. But tell me something. After your years in government investigation, what are you doing working in a boatyard?"

"I'm the majority owner of Silva's. The other partners like to keep my ship-disappearing story quiet. You know, Crazy Al and all that—not good for the boating business. Would you buy an expensive yacht from a nut? So, I'm doing what I love, which is hanging around boats and the water. I guess you want to know how I got my nickname. To get right to the point, yes, I did see a ship disappear—not sink, but disappear. I was transporting a boat from Santa Maria, one of the Azores islands, to deliver it to our yard here in Lisbon. We get to sell a lot of almost-new boats here. Some people with too much money in their pockets go out and buy an expensive yacht and then give up on boating after a couple of trips. One of the boats in the yard we originally sold new, and now it's listed for sale for the fourth time, and it only has 50 hours on the engine. Like I said, I love boats and the water, and I take jobs that I would normally farm out to a contractor or an employee. By the way, I'm licensed as a captain by the United States Coast Guard. Check it out."

"I will."

"Fucking spook," Al said with a laugh. "So, I was cruising in the 45-foot Hatteras when I came upon a beautiful ship named *Maltese*. It was after nine at night and dark, but the lights on the *Maltese* brightened things up. I cruised about 300 feet abeam of the ship on its starboard side. I actually had a radio chat with the captain on the bridge."

"Did you record the conversation, Al?"

"No, I didn't. I had no reason to. In the middle of our conversation, all hell broke loose, or at least that's how I perceived it. The area around the ship suddenly became bright daylight. It's hard to describe the event, especially because my heart was in my mouth when it occurred. Then I heard a thumping and rumbling coming from the ship's hull. I dropped the microphone, then picked it up to make a distress call to shore. I was amazed that I heard nothing coming from the *Maltese*. I shouted *Mayday, Mayday, Mayday,* the international distress signal. Before my call was answered, the bright daylight surrounding the ship became dark again—real dark because there were no lights from the ship. I'll admit that I was scared shitless, as we would say in the States.

"Assuming that the ship had sunk, I turned my boat toward her last position to cut through the wave that would be created when she went down. But there was no wave. The water was calm just like it was when I first saw the *Maltese*. The fucking thing just disappeared—not sank—just vanished from sight. At least I had the presence of mind to take an electronic fix, which I'll happily share with you. I continued to Lisbon, calling the Portuguese Coast Guard, the police, and just about anybody I could think of. I wasn't acting very professionally because I was totally freaked out. How the hell can a ship disappear?"

"And for simply reporting what you saw, you got the nickname, Crazy Al?"

"No, that was after the press got involved. An enterprising reporter from the *International Times* did some digging after our interview. About two years before the *Maltese Incident*, as it's come to be called, I wrote a novel, a lifelong dream of mine. In the novel, *The Punishing Sea*, a ship sank. It didn't disappear without a trace like the *Maltese*, it fucking sank in a storm. But the asshole from the *Times* saw an angle to sell newspapers. 'Crazy Al, the storyteller' was born. Word went through the publishing community that I made up a story about a fake event to sell my book. Of course, I didn't do that, but my book took off like a rocket. In retrospect it would have been a good idea to make up the incident just to sell books. So that's my story, Crazy Al's story, and I'm sticking with it."

"Al, you said that you took a navigational fix. Did you share it with the authorities?"

"I gave it to anyone who expressed an interest. I know that the US Coast Guard and the US Navy launched a search and rescue operation centering on my coordinates, but they found nothing. That only further enhanced my reputation as Crazy Al."

"So. you're the guy FBI Director Watson was talking about when she said she heard about a guy who saw the *Maltese* disappear. Have you gone back to the location yourself?"

"No fucking way. I haven't gone beyond the breakwater since the event. My love of water is now restricted to bays, rivers, and lakes."

"Al, have you heard about the sightings of that gigantic shark?"

"You'd have to be dead not to. It's all over the news. But what does a shark have to do with the *Maltese Incident*?"

"I don't know," I said. "I'm searching for clues, as I'm sure you can appreciate. The most recent news is that a 43-foot pleasure boat was attacked and sank, and four people were killed."

"That story gets me sick," Al said. "Silva's Boatyard is the local dealer for Grand Banks trawlers. I personally sold the boat to Steve and Grace Michaels. Really nice couple. They were looking forward to Steve's retirement and spending time on their beautiful trawler. What a fucking way to die."

"It's only a clue, and I don't know where I'm going with it. Al you've been tremendously helpful. Chances are strong that I may be in touch in the future. Anything else you'd like to add?"

"Yeah, I read all about Harry Fenton, the skipper of the *Maltese*. One of my partners served with him in the Navy. He's a hell of a guy from what I hear. Too goddam bad to lose a good man like him."

"You're right, Al. Fenton is, or was, a hell of a guy, and he's the main reason I've been assigned to this case. The president himself is quite fond of Harry Fenton."

CHAPTER TWENTY

Meg, Randy, and I sat in Randy's office for one of our many planning meetings. We liked to meet in Randy's office because it was large and had a pleasant view of the ocean.

"Wacky Bob Flowers approached me two days ago," Randy said. "He wants to meet with us to go over some ideas he's had."

"Hey, Randy, we shouldn't call him Wacky Bob," I said. "The guy's got one hell of a brain. What's his official title?"

"Chief Science Advisor. A lot of people think he's a bit nuts because he sits alone staring into the distance for hours at a time. But I think he's a solid character and is probably smarter than anybody else on the ship. Whenever Malta invested in a technology-based corporation, Bob would tie the company's people in knots with his due-diligence questions. If he wants to talk about something, we should listen."

"Bob Flowers is here," said Randy's assistant. "He said he's responding to your call."

"Good morning, Captain Fenton, Mrs. Fenton, Mr. Borg," Bob said.

"Relax with the formalities, Bob," I said. "Randy, Meg, and Harry will do. So, Randy says you want to share some ideas with us."

"I may have figured out a way for us to get back to where we came from," Bob said.

The room was silent except for Meg's coffee cup smashing to the deck. Randy handed Bob a cup of coffee but his hand was shaking so much that half of it spilled. Bob began to wipe the coffee off the table with a napkin.

"Hey, Bob, fuck the coffee," I said.

"You'll have to pardon Harry's language, Bob," Meg said. "But I must agree with him—Fuck the coffee and tell us about your idea for returning home."

"We got here for a reason," Bob said, "and I don't mean anything philosophical. We came to our state of affairs because something happened to the ship. Remember the deep darkness turning to daylight and the rumbling along our hull? Those events signified that something was happening, but we didn't know what. I think I've figured out what it was. It's frustrating without Google and the Internet to consult when you have a question. Therefore, I had to go from memory. People wonder why I'm often so quiet, but that's because I'm blessed with a thing called eidetic imagery, better known as a photographic memory. My brain files things that I've read, seen, or heard with the efficiency of the hard drive on a computer. But for a subject I didn't actively study, it sometimes takes a while for the images to pop up. That's why you see me sitting and staring a lot. I had never experienced that night-to-day phenomena, not to mention the rumbling along the hull, but I did recall *reading* about similar events. Once I remembered what I read, the memories flowed like water. I finally pieced together enough information from my different recollections to come to a conclusion."

"What?" the three of us yelled in unison.

"We've time-traveled."

"Bob, my friend," I said. "Just about everyone on this ship has arrived at that conclusion, not that any of us understands it. We've found no other human contacts, and most important of all, we've encountered dinosaurs, which are supposed to be extinct for millions of years. We all seem to know, without any scientific background, that we've somehow achieved the impossible —we've taken a trip from one dimension of time to another. So please tell us the details of your conclusion."

"All of your assumptions about time travel are missing an important element," Bob said, "how we did it. That's my breakthrough idea, I hope. In my past readings about time travel, which I'd mostly forgotten until I focused on them for a couple of days, there's a thing called a *wormhole* or time portal. You would need to be a physicist to understand the math behind it, but a wormhole is based on a concept in physics called an Einstein-Rosen Bridge, a portal from one time to another. Harry, you said that we did the impossible. But it only *seemed* impossible based on our knowledge and experience. It *is* mathematically possible to travel through time. Ask any theoretical physicist. And if it's mathematically possible to travel through time, it should be physically possible. Well, my friends, it is, and we've done it. Think about a wormhole as a funnel leading from one dimension to another. From my past readings I recalled that a wormhole occupies a definite location in time and space. There have been various reports over the years of a ship or vehicle going through a day-to-night or a night-to-day incident, and the events lasted for about two minutes. Sound familiar? And here is some positive news—time goes by a lot faster in the past, and we're living in the past. If we're able to get back, we'll find that we've hardly aged at all. That's wonderful news for my arthritic hip. Bottom line, if you can figure out where you came in, you can figure out how to go back. I'm going to guess that you took a navigational position when the ship hit the bizarre night/day event."

"Of course, I did. It's in my blood," I said. "Anytime something out of the ordinary happens, I take a fix. Yes, I took one for the night/day event. It's not precise because we were all busy freaking out, but it's close. So, Bob, are you telling us that all we have to do is cross over the same coordinates and voila—we're back to where we came from?"

"In a word, 'yes.' I know it's just a theory, but it's a theory on which I'm willing to bet my reputation. We need to go back to the coordinates of the wormhole."

The three of us sat there saying nothing, as if somebody just offered proof that Santa Claus exists. Then Meg stood and threw a binder full of papers into the air. She kissed Bob and Randy, and then threw her arms around my neck.

I wasn't cheering. I stood and walked over to the chart desk and calculated the distance from our current position to the place where the event occurred, the spot that Bob Flowers calls the wormhole. Then I then double-checked my numbers. I showed myself what I already knew.

"Hey, babe, you're not smiling," Meg said. "What's up?"

"You guys look to me for leadership and I hate to let you down. But I'm about to pour cold water on Bob's hot discovery—it won't work."

"I realize that I'm asking you to accept a theory that hasn't been proven," Bob said, "but every scientific bone in my body says that we can go home by passing through the wormhole, which is marked by the coordinates you recorded. What am I missing, Captain Harry?"

"*Fuel*, Bob. You're missing fuel. *We're* missing fuel. The coordinates you want me to cross are over 1,000 miles from here. We only have enough fuel to steam for 250 miles at best. I love your theory, but it won't work unless we can get there—which we can't."

CHAPTER TWENTY-ONE

At 6:30 a.m. the *Melody of the Seas* sounded its horn, waking half of Lisbon. Her bow and stern thrusters pushed her gently into the middle of the Tagus River, which led to the sea. Lars often missed the old days of tugboats nudging a ship into its cruising position. Bow and stern thrusters put a lot of tugboat people out of work.

"Forrest Sherman, Forrest Sherman, this is *Melody of the Seas,"* Captain Lars said over the radio. "Please come in."

"Hello, Lars, Jim Langdon here. We have our steaming directions and we're good to go. I'll keep station 1000 feet off your port stern. As we discussed, we'll leave our radios on, tuned to channel 12. If you find yourself being humped by a giant shark, I'll make a virgin out of him."

"I copy that, Jim. Glad you're along for the ride." Lars could breathe easier knowing that an American destroyer, armed with rockets, torpedoes, guns, and depth charges, would run interference for the *Melody of the Seas.* Would cruising at sea ever be the same? He wondered.

At 9 a.m. the two ships passed the breakwater and headed for the open ocean. As was prearranged by the captain of each ship, extra lookouts would be posted and sonar scopes would be continually manned.

At 10 a.m. Captain Lars introduced Father Rick Sampson, the ship's chaplain, an Episcopal priest who was on an anniversary cruise with his wife, Janet. Father Rick asked for silence.

"Ladies and gentlemen, let us bow our heads in prayer for the repose of the souls of the crew and passengers of the ship *Maltese,* which was last seen in these waters almost two months ago. In the name of our Heavenly Father, Amen."

Captain Lars turned to his first officer and said, "I can't believe it's been two months since the *Maltese* went missing, Bob. With no contact or evidence, we have to assume that the *Maltese* will never be found. A ship full of people—all dead, including my friend Harry Fenton. Damn shame. Two months is a long time."

CHAPTER TWENTY-TWO

"Ten years is a long time, Meg." We were in our room in Malta Town, preparing for a double anniversary party—our 10th wedding anniversary, and 10 years since we broke ground for Malta Town. Meg tightened the bow tie on my dress uniform.

"Damn. This collar has gotten awfully tight over the years. I remember when it fit perfectly."

I pinched Meg's bottom as she busied herself with my tie.

"Hey, stop that. I'm too fat to pinch."

"You're not fat, babe. You're a woman in full."

"We're both in full, honey. I'm 45 and you're 51 years old and we should watch our diets. Ever since Bob Flowers figured out how to make that delicious pasta our waistlines have been expanding. It seems like a few million years ago when we were in our thirties, both young, slim, and newly married."

"A few million years ago? That should explain the dinosaurs," I said. "Hey, we're still young. If it didn't take so goddam long to put this tux on, I'd say let's take our clothes off and get into bed."

"I'll take that as a date invitation, right after the party."

***

We held the celebration in "the ballroom," as we jokingly call it. The space is large, 50 by 75 feet, and was designed to accommodate full meetings as well as the occasional party. Malta Town consisted of 25 buildings carved up into separate apartments on a 20-acre plot, adjoining a 30-acre farm where we grew fruit and vegetables. We constructed a one-story hospital next to the housing units, designed with the help of Dr. Theresa. An electric fence surrounded both plots, thanks to Meg's foresight. Wally Bellino, the real estate development expert, drew up plans to allow for future growth. A key in designing space on Malta Town was that it be "defensible," because some of the dinosaurs hadn't gotten any friendlier. I laughed when I once asked Bellino what "DP" meant as noted on his blueprints. "Dinosaur-Proof," Bellino said.

Malta Town's climate is moderate, with an occasional high of 80 degrees Fahrenheit and a low of 60. Because we had no air conditioning, the moderate temperatures made life a little easier.

Randy Borg convinced me years ago to go through an election. They elected me Mayor of Malta Town, with over 99 percent of the vote. I would have gotten 100 percent, but I wrote in Meg's name when I voted. I won by a landslide mainly because I ran unopposed. Although I no longer have a ship under my command, everybody still calls me Captain Harry, which suits me just fine. Randy Borg is now 63 and as physically active as ever. The "triumvirate" of Meg, Randy, and me still exists after 10 years. So, I'm the mayor, and Randy and Meg are my council members, although I think of Meg as my deputy mayor. The three of us agreed, a few years back, that Malta Town needed some form of actual government, guided by a constitution, not by my whims.

The population of our little town includes 10 lawyers, whom I appointed to form a committee to draft a constitution. The United States Constitution, a copy of which we found in the ship's library, was used as a guide for the constitution of Malta Town. The committee agreed that they would draft the constitution in parts, writing first things first in order of need. The framers of the original United States Constitution wrote for their time and needs, and that's what the framers of the Malta Town Constitution did. They realized, for example, that the Interstate Commerce Clause wasn't necessary, so it disappeared from the to-do list. A lot of the United States Constitution was irrelevant to Malta Town, but significant parts were. They unanimously agreed on a First Amendment, guaranteeing freedom of speech and religion.

They also agreed that a Second Amendment was essential. The United States Constitution provided, in the Second Amendment, "A well-regulated Militia, being necessary to the security of a free State, the right of the people to keep and bear Arms, shall not be infringed." The words became part of the Malta Town Constitution, except for the part about "A well-regulated militia." Everybody in Malta Town carried a gun, so the committee figured they'd guarantee the right to bear arms. When you're attacked by a hungry *Velociraptor*, gun control is the last thing you want to think about.

The committee also realized that a constitution would be useless without a court system, and they provided for one. The court was comprised of Rebecca Flynn as Chief Judge, and two other lawyers who had experience in courtroom practice. Rebecca had served Malta Investments as in-house legal counsel. The members of the court also belonged to the 10-member constitutional committee.

A legislative committee consisted of ten people, all of whom had some experience working in a legislature, even if it was a school board. William Orlando, who had once served as supervisor of a suburban town of 300,000 people, headed the legislative committee. Because a town supervisor and a mayor have a lot of duties in common, I relied on Bill's advice over the years. At the first meeting of the legislative committee, all ten voted unanimously to elect an executive committee consisting of Meg, Randy Borg, and me. The committee also decided to hold only open meetings with no private executive sessions. They figured that openness was the most sensible way to ensure a robust, if small, democracy. The legislative committee worked closely with the constitutional committee.

The *Maltese* was now abandoned but still afloat in 75 feet of water. Two chains led from her hull to a large tree on the beach. Over the years, the ship provided Malta Town with a steady stream of supplies, especially the building materials and tools left by the former owner.

The tool shop was extensive, thanks to the foresight of the previous owner. The machine shop included metal lathes that we used to make wire for the electric fence to keep away hungry dinosaurs. The fence is the most crucial part of Malta Town. The manufactured wire, combined with Meg's fabulous idea of hydroelectric power from the nearby waterfall, made it possible for us to carve out our little civilization. Without the fence we'd all be items on a dinosaur buffet. The machine shop also made wire to bring electricity to all the housing units and other structures.

I knew that most of the people aboard the *Maltese* were smart, but I underestimated their ingenuity. A group of four people came up with a way to manufacture cement using local clay and limestone. We used the result to create foundations for the buildings as well as a septic system for each structure. We took the furniture from the *Maltese* and distributed the items among the various apartment units by lottery. Everybody agreed that I should own the captain's chair from the bridge. A group of three men and a woman made up the town's furniture-manufacturing group, replacing and adding to the existing stock as needed. The group consisted of talented amateur carpenters. Two of them were securities traders, one a programmer, and one was an accountant.

James Truesdale, who was Vice President of Security for Malta Investments, served as a New York City detective before he joined the company. We appointed him Chief of Police and assigned four people to serve with him as police officers. Crime was a minor issue in Malta Town. Truesdale and his "department" spent their time on domestic and neighbor disputes. We designated one of the administrative buildings as a "lockup." It was rarely used, except for the occasional citizen who had too much Malta Town distilled whiskey.

A committee of 10 made up the monetary commission. Jake Mendenhall, Senior VP for Finance for Malta Investments, headed the committee. Jake, who stood in as Meg's father at our wedding 10 years ago, is now 89 years old but mentally as sharp as ever. The committee included four economists, one of whom graduated from the University of Chicago, one from Columbia, and two from Stanford. Bob Flowers (Wacky Bob), Chief Science Advisor for Malta, was appointed to the committee, not for his knowledge of monetary policy, but for his overall intelligence and his memory. Meg, with an MBA from Harvard Business School, was also on the committee. A date was set three months in advance for the launch of Malta money, in denominations of "Malta

Dollars." The amounts would be set one week before launch, and the money would be distributed equally to each adult over the age of 18. One committee member wanted to peg the value of Malta Dollars to the price of gold, but he soon realized that we have no way to check its fluctuating value.

Currently, the Malta Town economy is based on barter. With a monetary system we expect to see the beginnings of a real free enterprise system. Soon, every resident of Malta Town would receive a regular monthly income. I suggested at a regular meeting, that because people would now have cash, we should set up *Brachiosaurus* races in a specially designed track. Meg gave me an elbow which she often does when I crack a bad joke.

Dinosaurs, our neighbors surrounding Malta Town, presented a serious problem, not so much for their ferocity, which was substantial, but for their stupidity. The giant *Brachiosaurs* never got the memo that the electric fence was designed to keep them *out*. During the building of the fence and for a long time after it was completed, *Brackos* (as we called them) regularly walked into the fence. When they received the shock, rather than retreat, the big dumb bastards pushed forward. Once a breach in the fence was opened, the *Bracko* would be followed by an assortment of local fauna, including the dreaded *Velociraptor*. Over a period of six months after the fence was "completed," three people were killed by the local critters, two by *Velociraptors*, and one by a *Tyrannosaurus*. Jim Truesdale and his four-man police force would be called any time a dinosaur incident occurred. Frank Murphy, the town's resident dinosaur expert, reminded Chief Truesdale that the animals are afraid of loud sounds. It took an enormous amount of ammunition to bring down a large dinosaur such as a *Bracko* or a *T-rex*, but the big beasts hated the sound of a shooting gun and the sting of the bullets. Large as they were, we managed to keep the local dinosaurs under control. *Velociraptors* were our biggest problem. Frank Murphy told anybody who would listen that *Velociraptors* are as intelligent as the smartest mammal. The fence maintenance people would find an answer to a safety problem, and then the *Velociraptors* would find a solution of their own. But as smart as they are, *Velociraptors,* too, are afraid of explosives and the sting of bullets. The executive committee (Meg, Randy, and I) decided to combat the problem by building lookout posts at six locations on the perimeter of the compound, much like guard towers around a prison. To save on ammunition, the guards would simply throw homemade firecrackers at the sight of an approaching animal. That system also kept the giant *Brachiosaurs* from stomping on the fence.

***

The band played and the room broke out in dance before the formal ceremony began. The eight- piece band, The Derivatives, played a sequence of popular dance songs from 10 years ago and longer. The band had been hired for the cruise. Little did they suspect that it would turn into a 10-year gig. When not playing, the band members taught music to anyone who wanted lessons. At Meg's urging, they planned to launch the first performance of a small symphony orchestra in less than a year. An accomplished cellist herself, Meg loved the idea and practiced regularly with the orchestra. She also gave me private lessons. Before long I loved to play the cello, thanks to Meg.

Just before the band leader introduced Randy Borg, the master of ceremonies, he led the entire group in *Show Me the Way to Go Home,* the theme song of Malta Town.

"Ladies and gentlemen," said Mike Malone, the band leader, "it's my pleasure and honor to introduce Randy Borg, CEO of what was one of the most successful investment companies on Wall Street. He's going to review some history of Malta Town, and maybe explain why nobody here has made a nickel in the past 10 years. After that, he'll introduce our guests of honor, celebrating their 10th wedding anniversary along with our community, Captain Harry and Meg Fenton, the hearts and souls of the *Maltese* and Malta Town."

Three *Brachiosaurs* were munching on leafy branches about 20 feet outside the compound near the ballroom. The *Brackos* heard a thunderous commotion coming from the building. People stood and yelled, and in some cases stomped their feet on tables, cheering for Meg and me. The *Brackos*, realizing that the cheering wasn't for them, strode as fast as they could in the opposite direction. The entire building shook and glasses tinkled from the sudden *Bracko* walk. Someone looked out a window and announced the departure of the three giants.

Randy, the master of ceremonies, waited for the cheering and laughing to stop.

"I'll be going through a reminiscence of our past 10 years in this community we call Malta Town," Randy said. "It's hard to imagine that this is the year 2027. But first I want to introduce two people whose wedding anniversary coincides with the anniversary of our town— Captain Harry and Meg Fenton, the George and Martha Washington of Malta Town. Both of these wonderful people have shown us what true leadership is."

"I wonder if Martha Washington was as good in bed as you, hon," I said, one hand over the microphone. Ouch. Elbow to the ribs.

"Let's hear it for our mayor, Captain Harry."

The cheering and yelling started up again. I raised the microphone, my other arm around Meg.

"There isn't a person in this room who doesn't want to return to the time and place where we came from." I said. More cheers followed. "That includes me, with one big exception. I don't want to be anywhere that my Meg isn't. She's beautiful, she's funny, and for the past 10 years, she's all mine. I can put up with anything—time travel, dinosaurs, dwindling supplies, but there's one part of life I can't do without—Meg. Even when she calls me nasty names."

Meg wiped a tear from her eye and wrapped her arms around my neck.

"Gimme a kiss, Dickbrain."

She didn't realize that the microphone was turned on and was near her mouth. The crowd burst out into laughs and applause. It would take a few weeks before people stopped calling me Captain Dickbrain. Meg later told me she had never been more embarrassed in her life. I thought it was the funniest thing I'd heard in years. *Captain Dickbrain, reporting for duty.*

The party continued until 3 a.m. Bob Flowers had long ago figured out a way to distill liquor, so the booze flowed freely. I turned to Randy and said, "What would we do without Bob Flowers?"

"Stay sober, for one thing."

"Goodnight, everybody," I said. "Here's to a great anniversary for a great community."

CHAPTER TWENTY-THREE

"Good morning, Buster," Captain Lars said. "Please join me for breakfast."

"Good morning, Captain. I think the *Melody of the Seas* is the perfect place to conduct my investigation. The breeze off the ocean opens my mind to clues."

When I came aboard the *Melody*, Captain Lars and I realized that we knew one another. Lars was a key witness in a terrorism case I worked on a few years ago. As a CIA agent, I felt uncomfortable as hell with people knowing my identity, but it's an inevitability we spooks live with.

"I find it interesting that we haven't seen one of those monster sharks after a full day at sea, captain. A few days ago we'd see one of the bastards every time we looked at the water."

"We're still in the Azores, Buster. There's hope yet. But as you've said before, a giant shark doesn't have anything to do with a ship disappearing."

"Our friend, Crazy Al from Lisbon, isn't so sure," I said. "Where is Al, anyway? It took a lot of persuasion to get him to take this cruise. You'd think he would be up here on deck."

"Hi guys," Al Avila said as he walked up to our table. "Sorry I 'm late for breakfast. She—I mean 'I'— decided to sleep late."

"That was one good-looking woman you were dancing with last night," I said.

"Yes, she certainly knows how to, uh, dance. So, any prehistoric shark sightings to tell me about?"

"Nothing, Al," I said. "I think this trip may be a waste of time."

"All you feds can think about is working on a case. Can't you just relax and enjoy yourself?"

"The day a spook doesn't chase down leads," I said, "is the day the spook evaporates. You're the biggest lead we've had so far, Al, somebody who actually saw the *Maltese* disappear. If we do encounter something, you'll help us figure it out. Chances are, you're the only person in the world who witnessed the dark turning to light and heard a ship rumbling."

I had already told Lars about the Al Avila story.

"Please take a seat," Captain Lars said. "Buster and I haven't eaten yet."

"If my calculations are accurate we should pass near the *Maltese* position at 9:33 tonight," Al said. "As I've said before, captain, I recommend that you give the position a wide berth. Yes, I took a fix that night, but because I was busy freaking out, I can't guarantee that it's accurate. The last thing we want to do is get gobbled up like the *Maltese* was."

"Don't worry, Al," Captain Lars said. "Although I'm not a superstitious man, I agree that we shouldn't take any chances."

"I really don't expect anything," Al said. The *Maltese Incident* will just be one of those unexplained events in life. So, tonight at 9:33 this ship will pass near the last known location of the *Maltese*. Please don't make it *too* near. It gives me the shakes thinking about it. Buster here wants me to join him on the upper deck at that time."

"Assuming you won't be busy with your newfound lady friend," I said with a wink.

"No problem, Buster. I think she's working her way down the passenger list."

***

"*Forrest Sherman, Forrest Sherman*, this is *Melody of the Seas*, over."

"Read you loud and clear, *Melody*."

"This is Captain Ragnarssen, may I please speak to Captain Langdon."

"Hello, Lars, Jim Langdon here. We seem to be in a megashark-free zone. We haven't seen one of those buggers so far, although we'll be in the Azores for another day. I'm assuming, of course, that the big sharks have some geographic relationship with the Azores, although I don't know for sure."

"Tonight at 9:33, Jim, we'll be near the location where the *Maltese* was last seen," Lars said. "I intend to be cautious and not steam too close to the location. We still don't know what happened to the Maltese, but whatever did happen, I don't want the *Melody* to have the same problem. There's a guy aboard who claims that he saw the *Maltese* disappear. He gave me the coordinates of the incident. I'm going to give the spot a wide berth."

***

At 9:05, Al and I stood on the upper deck, near an outdoor bar. Al ordered his second drink within 10 minutes.

"Maybe we should watch our drinking," I said. "In case something happens we want to have our wits about us."

"If we disappear," Al said, "I want to be good and fucking plastered to greet the event."

I looked at my watch.

"We're coming up on the mark. Captain Lars told me he's leaving a nautical mile between us and the coordinates of the incident."

"Ladies and gentlemen, this is the captain speaking. One mile off our starboard side is the location of the *Maltese Incident*. I thought you may want to make a note if you keep a diary."

The ship lurched to a sudden drop in speed, as if we hit something in the water. The sudden lurch was followed by a steady bumping sensation, shaking the deck and breaking glasses. The darkness was replaced by bright daylight.

"Holy shit," Al yelled. "I need another drink."

In two minutes, the darkness returned and the rumbling stopped. But the shouts from below decks continued. The ship was near panic.

"Dear God Almighty," Captain Lars said to First Officer Bob Simmons. "Get me Captain Jim on the *Forrest Sherman*."

"Forrest Sherman, Forrest Sherman, this is *Melody of the Seas,* over."

"Forrest Sherman, Forrest Sherman, this is *Melody of the Seas,* over."

"Forrest Sherman, Forrest Sherman, this is *Melody of the Seas,* over."

Bob Simmons looked at Captain Lars and said the obvious. "They don't answer, sir. The *Forrest Sherman* is no longer behind us."

Lars and Simmons stepped outside onto the open deck next to the bridge. It was dark, but there were no stars visible as there were a few minutes before. The sea was surprisingly calm. The men looked up at the sky and then at each other.

"Where the hell are we, Bob?"

"God knows, captain. I sure don't."

"Send out an announcement that I want to see Buster and Al Avila on the bridge."

Al and I entered the bridge as Bob Simmons was calling us.

Lars looked shaken. Who could blame him? Everybody on the ship, including me, was stunned.

"Mr. Avila, you're on record as having seen the *Maltese Incident*. Any comments?" Lars said.

"It looks like the fix I took that night wasn't accurate," Al said. "The light show and the rumbling were the same as the *Maltese Incident*, only closer. In answer to your next question, captain, I have no idea where we are."

"Captain, I recommend that you make an announcement to try to calm people down," First Officer Simmons said. "From all the shouting I hear, I think the passengers are on the verge of an emotional crack-up."

"Thanks for your input, Bob. I'll do that right away."

"Good evening ladies and gentlemen, this is Captain Ragnarssen speaking. The turbulence that we just went through is out of the ordinary, to say the least. With me on the bridge are some people who are familiar with this phenomenon. I will keep you up to date as events unfold, but I assure you there's nothing to be concerned about."

"I'd call that a gentle lie, captain," I said. "How long do you think it will keep things calm?"

"Not very long, I'm afraid, Buster" Lars said. "People want answers and I don't have any to give them."

"Who will tell the next story, captain?" asked Al Avila. "Please don't ask me to make an announcement explaining what happened. All I know is that this is the second time it happened, and this time I'm in it. Why don't you ask one of the bands to play?"

"You mean like on the *Titanic*?" Lars said, a smirk on his face.

"No sir, we're not sinking like the *Titanic,* but a little music may help people to calm down. They're frightened, captain, and so am I. How about drinks on the house?"

"Oh sure, take a thousand upset people and turn them into a thousand upset drunks," Lars said.

Master at Arms Ciano walked onto the bridge after asking permission. Dennis Ciano is the ship's "top cop." He's in charge of law enforcement and keeping the peace. Having once worked as a detective with the New York City Police Department, he was accustomed to large crowds—large unruly crowds.

"Fourth deck aft is secure for the time being, sir. People are talking and laughing."

"How did you pull that off, Dennis?" Lars asked.

"I decided it was time to start telling big stories. I told them that this phenomenon occurs all the time in April in the Azores, and that they should enjoy the new scenery. It's known among mariners as the *April Sky,* I told them. When people asked me about the rumbling I told them that whales like to mate near the surface in April. I also told them that daylight will be beautiful."

"Great," Al Avila said, "if it's like the daylight I saw around the *Maltese* it will look like spilled milk. Hey Dennis, if you ever want a job selling used boats, look me up."

"Thanks to our quick-thinking master at arms, we at least have a narrative to get us through a few days," Captain Lars said.

"A few days?" Al Avila said. "I remind you that the *Maltese* has been missing for two months."

"I don't care," said Captain Lars. "I can't get on the public-address system and announce that we have no idea what happened and no idea where we are. The passengers need to be told a story that will calm them down. Any thoughts, Buster?"

"I humbly disagree, captain," I said. "I've had some experience with crowd behavior. If you lie to them, they will eventually figure it out and then you'll be confronted by a bunch of angry people.. If you talk straight, they'll be upset but will gradually adjust to reality. The majority will turn to the panicked minority and reason with them. I've seen this happen. Don't worry, these people can handle a harsh truth. All they really need is an occasional update, even if nothing's new. But, typically, the captain, just like on an airplane, lets the passengers sit in ignorance of what's going on—and the passengers get pissed off."

"As the captain of this ship, it's my decision, of course. But I would like to see a straw poll among you concerning Buster's suggestion that I tell the complete truth as I know it. All in favor?"

Every hand went up, including Dennis Ciano's.

***

At 8 a.m., after a depressing milky daylight appeared, Lars picked up the microphone for the public-address system. Al Avila and I were next to him on the bridge.

"Remember, captain," Al Avila said, "the less bullshit the better."

"And remind them that they could have taken advantage of a free flight home a few days ago," Bob Simmons said. "What do you think, Buster?"

"Hell no," I said. "That would be picking a fight. They can figure out all on their own that they chose to stay on the ship."

"This is Captain Ragnarssen speaking. May I please have your attention?"

His last comment drew some laughs. Under the circumstances, nobody would dream of not giving the captain's words their full attention.

"Most of you will find what I'm about to say upsetting. That's understandable, because I find it upsetting myself. Some of our personnel have been telling people that the phenomenon we experienced was a thing called the *April Sky*. Well, although strange weather can accompany the month of April, what happened to us last night had nothing to do with it. You've heard about the widely reported disappearance of the American ship, the *Maltese*. Two months ago, the *Maltese* went missing and nothing has been found. It has become known as the *Maltese Incident*. A man who's aboard witnessed the disappearance of that ship, and he tells us that the phenomenon we experienced last night was similar to what happened to the *Maltese*. This afternoon at 2 p.m. we're going to meet in the main theater. Because many passengers chose to fly home a few days ago rather than wait for the home office to decide on a new itinerary, we can accommodate as many people who wish to attend. I strongly urge you to be there

CHAPTER TWENTY-FOUR

"Good afternoon, ladies and gentlemen, welcome to *Happening Now* with Jon Scott and me—Jenna Lee, for *Fox News*. You have probably already heard of the bizarre disappearance of the Norwegian Cruise Line ship the *Melody of the Seas*. Last night at 9:33 p.m., ship's time and local time in Portugal and 4:33 p.m. our time in New York, the *Melody of the Seas* suddenly disappeared. The American destroyer *USS Forrest Sherman* was steaming a half a mile behind the *Melody* when the cruise ship disappeared from sight. Captain James Langdon, commanding officer of the *Sherman,* said that he had the *Melody* in view a matter of seconds before it vanished. He and others on the destroyer reported a strange light surrounding the *Melody* just before it went missing.

"This event comes on the heels of another maritime incident just two months ago when the corporate cruise ship *Maltese* went missing in the same waters. No trace of the *Maltese* has been found, in what's become known as the *Maltese Incident.*

"The United States Navy and Coast Guard are on the scene conducting a massive search-and-rescue operation. Let's hope they find more than they did while searching for the *Maltese.* The search-and-rescue operation for the *Maltese* is now a search operation only. The significance of that decision is obvious—they don't expect to find any survivors of that tragedy.

"Norwegian Cruise Line, the owner of the *Melody of the Seas*, reports a 92 percent cancellation rate just since last night. Other cruise ship companies, including Carnival, Celebrity, and Viking, report similar cancellation numbers. People are starting to see cruising as a dangerous way to vacation.

"Just a few days ago I reported another strange series of events involving the *Melody of the Seas.* The ship's captain reported multiple sightings of a giant shark known as a *Megalodon*—a fish that was thought to be extinct. Photographs taken by passengers and crew add reality to the reports. I'm asking our camera man to zoom in on some of these photos. You can see how terrifying it must have been to stand on a ship and see these monsters in the water.

"Our guest this afternoon is Mr. Mike Fletcher, speaking to us from Norwegian Cruise Line headquarters in Brandon, Florida. Mr. Fletcher is a former sea captain and a professional maritime disaster investigator.

"Mike, give us your take on these strange goings on," Jon Scott said.

"Good afternoon, John and Jenna," Fletcher said. "These events are strange, indeed. I was the full-time investigator for the *Maltese Incident*, and the event is still in my active folder. The disappearance of the *Melody of the Seas* has me completely stumped, I must admit. I was scheduled to be on the *Melody* to confer with her captain, Lars Ragnarssen, when I was abruptly summoned back to Florida by Norwegian Cruise Line management. If it weren't for my meeting at headquarters, I would have disappeared along with the *Melody*. There doesn't seem to be a ready explanation, just as with the *Maltese Incident*. Although the search-and-rescue operation has just begun, we fear that we may find the same result as we did with the *Maltese*—not only couldn't we find the ship, we were unable to find any debris or metallic sounds to tell us where the ship went down. Another part of this strange story is that both ships went missing in the same area of ocean in the Azores."

"Mike, I'm sure we'll be speaking again soon. Good luck with your investigation."

"Something very strange is going on in the ocean around the Azores, ladies and gentlemen, and nobody seems to know what. Jenna Lee reporting for *Fox News*."

CHAPTER TWENTY-FIVE

"Do you miss being a sea captain, honey?" Meg asked me.

Meg and I walked the property of Malta Town the day after the big anniversary party, not just for exercise, but to discuss plans for the future of the community.

"Yes, I definitely miss being a sea captain. It meant having a place to go, a destination. I could tie up or drop anchor, and there was a whole new world wherever I went. I'm not happy being in one place. If it weren't for you, I think I'd go nuts."

We stepped behind a tree and kissed. Meg's rifle strap slipped off her shoulder.

"Hey, babe, keep that rifle dinosaur-ready."

"So, to change the subject, how did you like the party last night?" Meg said as she readjusted the AR-15 on her shoulder.

"I thought it was great. I still can't believe that we've been here 10 years and that we've been married that long. And don't make a crack about time flying when you're having fun."

"I was just about to make that very crack. You and I have gotten to reading each other's minds. So tell me, Mr. Landlocked Captain, how do you think our community is doing?"

"That's the only good part about not being at sea—we live in a good place, populated by great people. I don't know if it's a thing called chemistry, but I find our neighbors to be the best I could choose to live with, and you're the best of the best. Maybe adversity does bring out what's good in people."

"Would you trade it for something else if you could?" Meg asked.

"Except for you, Meg, I would change all this bullshit in a prehistoric minute to go back to the civilization we came from. You're the best thing that ever happened to me, back where we came from, or now. But I sure as hell would like to go back. You?"

"Yes, it would be great to be back in our old—or is it new—world," Meg said. "And we're not the only ones. A lot of our people left behind spouses, lovers, children, and grandchildren. Every now and then I get into a conversation with one of them, and the mood turns sad. A lot of our friends and neighbors feel stranded. We're all proud of what we've built, but I think we'd all give it up to go back."

"Some of them have moved on," I said. "I mean they've moved on in their heads. Ten years away from their families takes a toll, but people adjust. Look at how many people paired off and became couples like you and me. We were single, so we just began out of the starting gate."

"Let's talk about Bob Flowers and his big idea," Meg said.

"Bob's idea of going forward in time is a great concept," I said, "but without fuel it will remain just an idea. Last week I spoke to him about turning his brain loose on making fuel. He pointed out that first, we need to find oil, and then we have to figure out how to turn it into diesel fuel. Another problem is the *Maltese* herself. Let's face it, our ship is a rusted-out hulk, with all her moveable parts stiff or useless from age, salt, and moisture. I even thought about building a sailboat. I didn't bring it up because you'd think I was nuts. I spoke to our carpenters, and they all agreed that the wood here is not good for building something that floats. It's okay for land structures, but it's too porous for waterproof planking, and we don't have tar for the joints. Besides that, nobody aboard is skilled in maritime carpentry. We're stuck here, babe. We've made the best of it so far, and my way of thinking is to continue to improve our lives among the dinosaurs. They may be bigger than us, but we're a hell of a lot smarter than them. We've come up with quite a decent little town. We've set up a judicial system, law enforcement, farming, and, thanks to you, we even have a softball league and pretty soon a symphony orchestra."

"Harry, you sound like you're talking yourself into liking it here more than you do. After 10 years I think I know you, and something tells me that you feel stuck, despite our nice little town."

"It's a good thing I love you, Meg, because there's no way I could keep anything from you, even when it's me doing the thinking."

"Hey, let's walk through the farm," Meg said. "We can pick a couple of those wonderful apples from that tree in the orchard."

As we walked through the gate leading to the farm, I glanced up at one of the lookout towers.

"Why the hell is that tower unmanned?" I yelled, to no one in particular.

"Maybe the lookout had to climb down to take a tinkle, Meg said. "Oh shit—Harry turn around," she screamed.

A six-foot *Velociraptor* charged us. Meg slung her rifle into firing position, dropped to one knee, and pumped three rounds into the attacker's torso, killing him. His lifeless body fell three feet in front of us.

"Let's climb the tower, Meg. Keep your rifle handy."

We climbed the ladder to the lookout platform. When we got to the top, we heard a sound and looked down. Four *Velociraptors* were gathered at the base of the tower.

"Hands over your ears, hon," Meg yelled. She opened the ammunition locker and grabbed a hand grenade. "Hi, sweeties, come to mama," she shouted as she dropped the grenade into the group of hungry raptors. One of them grabbed the grenade in its mouth, blowing its head off. I shot the other three. I made a quick mental note that we need to make more grenades for just such an occasion.

"We need to make more grenades for an occasion like this," Meg said, duplicating my thought exactly.

"Great idea, hon," I said. "Why didn't I think of that?"

I held the radio to my mouth and yelled, "Guard shack, this is Captain Harry, come in."

"Hello captain, what's up?" answered the man on duty.

"Guard tower number four on the northeast section of the farm is unattended," I said. "Also, there's an apparent breach in the fence. We've killed a total of five raptors. I can see the breach in the fence from here, about 50 feet south of tower four. Send a guard patrol and fence repair crew and keep your weapons in firing position. Meg and I are in the tower and we'll direct you from here and give you cover. I see an object next to the fence breach that looks like a human body."

Meg tapped my arm and pointed as I spoke on the radio. She was pointing at six more raptors approaching the tower.

"They're walking slowly, hon," Meg said. "I think they're looking for their next meal. I'll shoot the one on the right and work inward, so you can shoot the one on the left and do the same."

We killed all six raptors.

"All the gunfire should keep any other intruders away for a while," I said. "How's your ammo, babe?"

"I've got three rounds in the gun and another 12 in a spare magazine. That should hold us until the others get here."

Six people, known as a *guard patrol*, entered the farm, followed by a fence repair crew of four. They walked cautiously, sweeping their heads from left to right as they had been trained by Dom Maslow, the former soldier. The group leader was Loretta Jones, who once served Malta as a tax attorney.

"Hey Meg, remind me to put out a memo that anyone serving guard tower duty can't leave the tower unless someone with a gun is standing by," I said. "How are you doing, hon?"

"Oh, nothing like being attacked by a few raptors to make for a pleasant morning."

We held our rifles at the ready to provide cover for the guard patrol and fence repair crew while we waited for the regular person on watch to relieve us in the tower.

"Hey what's all the shooting about?" Loretta Jones asked. "Nice way to aggravate a goddam hangover."

"We were just making nice with a few *Velociraptors*," Meg said.

The replacement for watch tower four, Bill Blankenship, climbed up the ladder.

"That body over there is Dave Norton," Blankenship said. "I was due to replace him, but I guess he wanted to inspect the fence breach without waiting. I recommend that you send out one of your no-shit security memos, Harry. Walking without a rifle should be strictly forbidden. I think we should change the Second Amendment of our Constitution from a right to bear arms to a *duty* to bear arms. Hey, nice shooting, Meg."

I radioed Stu Riordan, Malta Town's chaplain, to arrange for a funeral for Dave Norton. Stu isn't a clergyman, but a deeply religious guy. He didn't hesitate when, years ago, I asked him to serve as our chaplain.

Meg and I walked back through the gate leading to the main compound.

"I've had enough excitement for the morning, Harry. Why don't we continue our conversation about how much fun it is to live in Malta Town?"

"Let's do lunch," I said. "Being attacked by hungry dinosaurs always gives me an appetite."

We entered one of the two diners on the compound. Nobody knew what to call the eating establishments, so they became known as diners. They were imaginatively named by the infrastructure committee as The North Diner and The South Diner. The food also tastes like it was put together by a committee. When we first came ashore 10 years ago we hoped to find edible small game besides fruit and vegetables. We did find some edible game, including small ungulates that looked like deer, but there was one problem—the meat was tough as hell and they all tasted horrible. So, although we're ashore, fish is the highlight of any menu.

"I'm looking forward to the day when we print money," I said. "Once we can exchange currency we'll start to see business activity replace this forced socialism. There's nothing like free enterprise to deliver satisfaction, including tasty food."

"Hey, hon, look at the bright side," Meg said. "No hungry dinosaur would set foot in one of these places."

We sat at a table by a window with a great view of the forest. Too bad the view isn't edible. The waiter, Jimmy Reese, came to the table. Jimmy was once a computer programmer with Malta Investments. The Infrastructure Committee also determined that table-waiting would be a rotating assignment, the result of which was that nobody gained any table service skills.

"Hi Harry, hi Meg. Our specialty today is—surprise—fish. But I'm happy to announce that there's a choice. We can fry it, bake it, or serve it raw. Hey, what's that smell?"

"Maybe it's your latest catch of fish," Meg said.

"No, I think it's outside. It smells like something's burning," Jimmy said.

The three of us went out to investigate.

"It's that shed by the farm where they keep cans of wood stain," Jimmy said. I couldn't believe that we still had wood stain from the *Maltese* after 10 years. But, judging from the burning shed, there was now a lot less.

As we spoke, a group of people wheeled up and unrolled a fire hose, one of the valuable items we retrieved from the *Maltese*. The nearby waterfall, besides acting as a source of hydroelectric power, provided a water system with pipes throughout Malta Town. The pipes were salvaged from the *Maltese*. The fire fighters hooked up the hose to one of five fire hydrants in the town, smothering the burning shed in water. After five minutes, the fire was out, but the smoke kept billowing into the air.

"Your firefighting training paid off, hon," Meg said. "Those guys handled that hose like they do it for a living."

"Damn, that thing is smoky," Jimmy said.

"Yeah," I said. "It masks the smell of that crap you're cooking."

"Maybe the smoke will attract a rescue party to come save us," Meg said.

"You're becoming a bigger wiseass than me," I said.

CHAPTER TWENTY-SIX

"Let's hear it for Rick Townsend, the Entertainment Officer of the *Melody of the Seas,*" said the band leader.

A smattering of weak clapping followed his announcement.

"Ladies and gentlemen, I normally stand in front of you with my bright smile, cracking bad jokes, and giving you confusing tour instructions. As the Entertainment Officer, my job consists of light and airy fun stuff. But this afternoon, we need to address some important matters. Have you noticed?"

He was amazed that his crack actually brought some laughter.

"It gives me great pleasure to introduce The Man with the Answers. Well, let's just say he's The Man. Ladies and gentlemen, the commanding officer of the *Melody of the Seas*, Captain Lars Ragnarssen. He's an expert fisherman, and after his question and answer presentation, Captain Ragnarssen will deliver his popular lecture, 'How to Catch a Prehistoric Shark.'"

Lars had mixed feelings about Rick Townsend's humor, but he figured it couldn't hurt, and may even warm up a tense situation.

"Ladies and gentlemen," Lars began, "two nights ago we experienced something out of science fiction. We went from darkness to sudden daylight, and the ship rumbled as if we were steaming over cobblestone. As I said in my brief announcement, there are two questions that I know you want to ask.

"First, what happened? The answer is, we don't know. Second, where are we? The answer to that question is also, we don't know.

"Yes, I understand that we should be able to answer those questions, but unfortunately we can't. So now I'm going to open the floor to any questions. I'll answer your questions fully and truthfully, to the extent that I know the answer. If I don't know it, we'll try to find the answer."

"Captain, my name is Hank Billings from Tulsa, Oklahoma. I'm a petroleum engineer. My question is: How far we can travel on the amount of fuel that's aboard?"

"We topped off in Lisbon, Mr. Billings," Lars said. "We can travel at moderate speed for about 5,000 miles. We have one of the largest fuel capacities afloat, so we have plenty of cruising range, but I don't know where we'd go."

"Sir, my name is Walter Roemer from Chicago, where I work as a stockbroker. You said that you don't know what happened or where we are. Fair enough, but what are you going to do to answer those questions?"

"Mr. Roemer, that is a fair question, probably the best question that anybody could ask. It could be summarized as 'now what?' The answer is that we are headed toward the land that you can see on the horizon dead ahead, although it doesn't appear on any of our charts. If the stars come out, we can take a celestial fix, but it won't do us much good without accurate charts. I want to put out the word that we welcome input from all of you, although that isn't what you paid for. Speaking for myself and my crew, we want to go home as much as you folks."

"Captain, my name is Dwight Thurber. I live in New York City and I'm a professor of paleontology."

"Paleontology?" said Captain Lars. "That would be the study of prehistoric fossils, is that correct Mr. Thurber—or is it *Doctor* Thurber?"

"Yes, it's Doctor Thurber, but you can call me Ike, captain. A colleague of mine, a Doctor Max Feigenbaum, is actually in Lisbon as we speak. He's investigating the numerous sightings of the giant shark, the *Megalodon*. He conferred with me while this ship was in port. So, my question is, have we had any sightings of the *Megalodon* since we left Lisbon?"

"No, we haven't, Ike. We've been at sea for two days without one sighting. I can't explain it, nor can I explain if a prehistoric fish has anything to do with our current circumstances. If we do see any more giant sharks, I'll be calling on you."

"Captain, my name is Jake Monahan and I'm a retired junior college teacher from Long Island, New York. My son is a novelist, or fancies himself to be one. Only kidding. He writes well, and I think his books are great. His favorite genre is time travel, and all five of his books involve that theme. So, here's a completely insane question: Do you think we've traveled through time?"

"Mr. Monahan, your question isn't insane," Lars said. "Until we can find a more logical answer to our circumstance, your question is quite reasonable. If you ask me if we're all characters in a Disney cartoon, I would be willing to entertain the possibility."

***

I walked along the promenade deck feeling like a spooked-out spook. I was with my new friend, Al Avila.

"Hey, Buster, have I thanked you recently for inviting me on this lovely cruise?"

"Okay, wise guy, I'm no happier than you are to be here. Let's stop complaining and start thinking."

"I don't want to think about being stuck on this ship indefinitely, but you're right, we need to think."

Al stood there and did nothing.

"What are you doing?" I asked.

"I just did some thinking and I haven't come up with anything. I believe it's more productive to complain."

"I wonder if the sun ever shines or if we're stuck in this permanently cloudy weather," I said, changing the subject. "This may sound weird, but it seems like we're in a gigantic cave."

"Nothing sounds weird given our circumstances, Buster. Even the ocean looks weird. Holy shit, look at that. Is that our friend the giant shark? And there's another one."

I picked up a house phone hanging on a bulkhead and reported our double shark sighting to the bridge. Al snapped photos with his phone.

"This is the first officer speaking. We've seen the sharks from the bridge, Mr. Atkins. Thank you for your report."

"Mr. Atkins?" Al said. "Your mailman must have schizophrenia."

"It's one of my CIA aliases. Remember—my very existence is top secret. How am I doin?"

"Your secret is safe with me, Buster. With me and about half the ship."

"Hey look, Buster, I think I see another one of the giant sharks about 200 feet to starboard."

"Forget the shark," I yelled. "Look at that smoke off the starboard bow. There's no electric storm going on, so it can only mean one thing. People start fires. There must be people ashore."

CHAPTER TWENTY-SEVEN

The atmosphere aboard the *Melody of the Seas* became one of pandemonium once word got around that smoke could be seen ashore. The chance of possible human contact swept through the ship like a fresh breeze.

Al and I went to the bridge to personally report the fire to Captain Lars.

"Do you two know anything about fires, Buster?" Lars asked.

"I'm trying to remember the name of a guy from Detroit I met the other day," I said. "Maxwell, yes that's his name, Frank Maxwell. He's a retired fire chief."

The first officer picked up the phone and announced, "Mr. Frank Maxwell, please report to the bridge."

Maxwell walked onto the bridge, stumbling over a stool as he stared at the fire ashore.

"It's strange to look at that fire without the sound of sirens," Maxwell said. "I feel like I should be in uniform."

"Mr. Maxwell, I understand that you're a retired fire chief," Captain Lars said. "Please describe that fire."

"I'm sure it's a chemical fire, probably paint or more likely wood stain or turpentine from the looks of the thick smoke. If we were within a mile of the fire you could smell it."

"So, you think the fire is man-made?" I asked.

"I can't tell how it was set, of course," Maxwell said, "but I'm sure the fuel is man-made, most likely chemical in origin. Fires like that usually happen by spontaneous combustion because some jerk packed a locker too tight with wood stain, rags and other combustible. Also, from the billowy nature of the smoke, it looks like somebody hosed it down. As a matter of fact, it may no longer be a fire, just the water-soaked remnants of one. From the way our bow is pointed, captain, it looks like we're going to have ourselves a closer look."

"Yes, we are, Mr. Maxwell. Please remain on the bridge to help us with your knowledge."

"Oh my God, what's that?" Maxwell yelled, pointing to the left.

Lars looked through a high intensity telescope and focused on the object Maxwell pointed to.

"That, ladies and gentlemen, is a ship," Lars yelled. "The name on her hull is *Maltese.*"

***

After making sure the fire was safely extinguished, Meg and I decided to skip the fish and munch a couple of apples down by the ocean. The electric fence didn't extend all the way to the water, but terminated about 50 feet from the edge, near the top of a berm. A gate led to the water, with a switch to turn the current on and off. The rule in Malta Town was to avoid walking near the water unarmed because there was no electric fence to deter dinosaurs.

We stood on top of the berm enjoying the wind from the ocean, which blew away the smoke from the paint locker fire.

Meg spit out a chunk of apple.

"Oh my God, I don't believe it, Harry," Meg screamed, grabbing my arm. "Can I really be seeing that? Please tell me it's not my imagination."

"What do you see, hon, a *Megalodon*?"

"Harry, just look, straight ahead." She handed me her binoculars.

The *Melody of the Seas* appeared majestically about two miles from our position, heading straight for us.

"Holy shit," I observed.

"Somehow I knew you'd say that, Harry."

I had the same feeling that I had over 10 years ago when we went through the wormhole. I couldn't believe what I was seeing.

"It's heading in this direction, Harry. We can't see the name from the side, but it looks like one of those huge new cruise ships."

I looked at Meg and smiled. "I bet she carries a lot of fuel."

"Enough to get to that wormhole thingy that Bob Flowers spoke about?"

"Hey, Meg, what the hell are we doing standing here talking? We need to attract that ship."

I took the radio from my belt.

"Malta Town Headquarters, this is Captain Harry, come in."

"This is Jim Valente, go ahead, Harry."

"You won't fucking believe it, Jim, but Meg and I are on the beach looking at a big cruise ship heading our way. Grab as many signal flares as you can and tell anybody you see. We need to go outside the fence to the water line, so make sure you send at least two Guard Patrols to protect us from animals and help with the boat. We want to welcome that big ship in style. I don't know the ship's name but I'll try to get her on my radio."

"Just call her anything, Harry. I'm sure they don't get much radio traffic."

"Any vessel, any vessel, this is Captain Harry Fenton of the ship *Maltese*, come in please."

The bridge on the *Melody* erupted in screams.

"Harry, great to hear your voice, my friend. This is Lars Ragnarssen on the *Melody of the Seas*. I read you loud and clear. The world has been wondering what happened to you folks. Now they're wondering what happened to us."

"Lars and I had a few drinks after a training seminar," I said to Meg. "He's a good guy."

I had a hard time hearing Lars through the pandemonium on the *Melody*'s bridge.

"Lars, how the hell are you? A few of us are coming out to meet you. We have a lot to talk about."

Our motor launch had long ago run out of fuel, so we all pulled on oars.

Randy Borg and Bob Flowers joined Meg and me. We all rowed in unison and pulled up next to the ship within minutes. It would have been easier to simply wait for one of the ship's motor launches to come to us, but we wanted to see the *Melody* up close. The deck crew lowered the boat platform on the starboard side of the ship. One of the *Melody* crewmen escorted us to an elevator that took us to the bridge. When we entered the bridge, everybody cheered so loud it actually hurt my ears. Wait till they come to Malta Town, I thought.

Lars looked at the gray hair that was sprouting on my head.

"I see you've grown some gray hair, Harry. I guess the stress of the last two months aged you a bit."

"Last two months?" I shouted. "Lars, we've been here for 10 fucking years. Meg and I just celebrated our 10th wedding anniversary. Did I misunderstand you?"

"Harry, what date do you think this is?" Lars asked as he sat down, his face suddenly pale.

"April 20, 2027. Why do you ask? What date do *you* think it is?"

"Harry, I don't know how to break this to you, but today is June 15, 2017. The *Maltese* has only been missing for two months."

I pointed to the rusty hulk of the *Maltese*, still anchored in shallow water.

"Lars, does that ship look like it's been gone for two months? It's a rusting pile of metal. We stripped every useful item from the ship and used the stuff to build Malta Town."

"Malta Town? You built a compound on land? In just two months?"

"Well, it took a couple of years. Despite the dinosaurs we managed to build a town."

"Dinosaurs? You've got to be kidding me," Lars said. "Are you telling me that dinosaurs inhabit this land?" He turned to look at Dr. Thurber, the paleontologist. "Ike, would you like to comment?"

"My God," said Thurber, "that could explain our sightings of the *Megalodons*."

"We were bumped by one of those monsters before we went through the crazy event," I said.

"By 'crazy event,' I guess you mean the night becoming day and a rumbling along the ship's hull," Lars said. "That's exactly what happened to the *Melody*. What happened to you folks has become known as the *Maltese Incident*. It's a worldwide sensation—a ship that simply disappeared. They're still searching for the *Maltese*, but have pretty much given up hope."

"A scientist in our group told us that the strange light and bumping event was caused by crossing a time portal, also known as a wormhole. That, according to Dr. Bob Flowers, the man standing next to me, is how we've travelled through time."

"Traveled through time?" Lars said. "Do you think it's too early for me to have a drink?"

All of us at Malta Town have had 10 years to adjust to our new surroundings, which aren't new anymore. Captain Lars and the people on the bridge of the *Melody* looked like they'd been struck by lightning. Shock doesn't describe the look on their faces. I can imagine what my face looked like. I glanced down at Meg, who was hugging me so tight it's as if she thought I'd blow away.

"So now there's a *Melody Incident*," I said. "Welcome to our club. But let me change the subject, Lars. How much fuel do you carry?"

"Close to 5,000 gallons. We topped off before we left Lisbon. Why do you ask?"

"I'll let Bob Flowers explain his theory," I said.

"To make it simple, captain," Bob Flowers said, "I believe that we can get back to where we came from by steaming across the exact location we hit when the event occurred. We didn't have enough fuel on the *Maltese*, so that's why we haven't tried it. As Harry said, it's called a wormhole or a time portal, a key part of the science behind time travel. That's what happened to all of us. We've time traveled, every one of us. I'm 65 years old, and I look forward to going back to when I was 55."

"Bob," Meg said. "I've heard you say it before, but please repeat yourself. Are you saying that we'll be 10 years younger when we cross that wormhole thing?"

"Yes, that's exactly what I'm saying. We'll travel back to 2017. I look forward to attending your wedding—again."

Lars mopped his brow. I wiped mine.

"Here's a big question, Lars," I said. "We started out with 1,050 adults but are down to 1023 after a few deaths. Add to that 178 children. Can you accommodate that many people? people? If you look at the *Maltese*, you can see that she's obviously not seaworthy. We don't need luxury quarters, just a place to rest our heads."

"We've got plenty of room, Harry. We left behind 1,200 people in Lisbon who chose to fly home rather than wait for our home office to make up its mind about our itinerary."

"If Bob's theory doesn't work," I said, "we can expand Malta Town and you can move ashore with us. Dinosaurs can be fun if you leave them alone."

Lars just stared at me, apparently not excited by the prospect of living among dinosaurs.

CHAPTER TWENTY-EIGHT

William Orlando, the Speaker of the Malta Town legislature, called the meeting of 20 legislators to order. He banged his gavel, which consisted of a carpenter's hammer and a block of wood.

"Hello, everyone," Orlando said. "In view of the work in front of us, can I hear a motion to suspend the reading of the minutes from the last meeting? I'm as excited as anyone else here, so pardon me if I step on a few words. We're happy that our captain, mayor, and good friend, Harry Fenton, is with us this morning, along with his lovely wife, Meg. I've also invited Rebecca Flynn, the Chief Judge of the Malta Town court, and Randy Borg, CEO of Malta. This is a special meeting of the Malta Town Legislature, and with any kind of luck, it will be the last. You all know the details of the past few days. The ship *Melody of the Seas* has graced our shores and brought with her, praise be to God, our possible ticket home. With a hell of a lot of diligence on the part of a lot of people, we've put together a functioning town, with a legislature and a court. We operate under a constitution that we've tailor made to our circumstances, as a small group of people living among the dinosaurs. Because we've all agreed to operate under the laws as enacted, I've called this special meeting."

"Let's hear it for Bill Orlando," Rebecca Flynn announced as she stood up and clapped. Everyone laughed and applauded because Judge Flynn had just used the Malta Town traditional method to get the loquacious Bill Orlando to shut up and get to the point.

"Okay, I can take a hint," Orlando said, laughing, "and here's the reason for this meeting. The next few days will be totally different from our past 10 years. As we pack our meager belongings and move aboard the *Melody of the Seas* for our journey home, we need to change our system of laws. If we don't we'll probably find ourselves in constant violation of law and waste a lot of time before Judge Rebecca. We need to move fast, and make decisions quickly. Therefore, as we've discussed in committee, I'll entertain a motion to suspend the laws of Malta Town and give all decision-making power to our mayor, Captain Harry Fenton."

After he heard a second, Bill Orlando said, "Discussion on the motion?"

Rebecca Flynn's hand shot up.

"Although I'm not a member of the legislature, I would like to comment on this motion unless somebody objects. Vesting all power in a single individual is normally a terrible idea, especially in our little democracy. But under the rapidly changing circumstances, and because Bill Orlando asked that power be vested in the finest gentleman in Malta Town, I support this motion. We long ago elected Harry as our mayor, but to us he'll always be known as Captain Harry. I urge everybody to vote 'yea' on the motion. We can count on Meg being at his side to help him, and hopefully curb his colorful language."

"You can fucking count on it, Becky," I said from the back of the room. Meg delivered an elbow to my ribs.

Everyone cracked up as one legislator shouted, "Move the question."

The motion carried unanimously.

"And now a word from our fearless leader, Captain Harry," Orlando said.

"It's no exaggeration that I love you guys," I said. "I don't think you'll need a captain, or a mayor for that matter, because we'll be guests on somebody else's ship. So, you've honored me with this temporary position because we need to make a lot of fast decisions. As soon as we're all aboard the *Melody*, I will step down from my position in favor of Captain Ragnarssen. We've gotten to know each other in the past 10 years, or two months according to the *Melody* people, and therefore I give you my solemn pledge—I'll try not to screw it up. I'm going to say something that I only dreamed about over the years—we're going home. Hey, let's go, we've got moving to do."

***

After a discussion with Captain Ragnarssen, Randy agreed to lead group tours of passengers from the ship, showing them how a thousand people created a thriving town in a forest full of nasty animals. First Officer Jim Valente and Frank Murphy, the dinosaur expert, agreed to help him. They used four motor launches from the *Melody*, each capable of carrying 25 passengers, so the total tour operation of 1,200 people at two tours a day would take six days, enough time to enable the residents of Malta Town to pack our belongings and board the *Melody*. I assigned 10 extra people to armed guard duty. We wouldn't want to lose any of our new friends to a hungry dinosaur. I called a general meeting in the "ballroom" to discuss the plans for moving to the ship.

"Hello everybody," I said. "It's safe to say that we're all as excited as hell. In a few days we're going to test Bob Flowers' theory of time travel and go back to where we came from. But first we need to discuss an orderly move from our land-based home in Malta Town to our new temporary home, the *Melody of the Seas*. Captain Lars told me that the *Melody* is traveling light with only 1,200 passengers and a small crew. That leaves plenty of room for us. But we can't take all our belongings, so please make careful choices on what to bring. If anybody wants to bring aboard some dinosaur souvenirs, and Dr. Bob Flowers thinks it's a good idea, please take nothing bigger than a *Velociraptor skull*. We estimate that the move will take six days. I appointed a team of 10 moving supervisors, so direct any questions or problems to one of them. Each supervisor will be wearing a large badge that reads, 'Homeward Bound.' Hey, we carved a civilization out of a forest, so moving to the ship should be easy. When you go aboard the *Melody*, please follow the instructions of the crew. They will first lead you to a huge auditorium where we'll be given inoculations in case we picked up some jungle rot that we don't know about. Any questions?"

"Harry, it's been 10 years since any of us saw money," Jim Valente said. "I'm sure Randy doesn't want to drop off a bunch of broke and homeless securities dealers."

"I talked to Randy about exactly that. Remember, we're going to travel back to 2017. We'll only have been gone for a little over two months from that year. Although he may no longer be CEO, he is a major voting shareholder and his word carries a lot of clout. I'm sure the board will reappoint him as CEO anyway. Randy figures that Malta will pay your salaries back to the date we disappeared, plus any incidental expenses such as late mortgage payments. Malta was a thriving investment company when we left, and I'm sure it couldn't go downhill in a couple of months. Captain Lars tells me that the stock market's been in bull territory since we left, so I really wouldn't worry about money. We've all been on a bizarre forced saving plan."

"Harry, can you give us a rough idea of timing?" Dom Maslow asked.

"Hey, Dom, you're talking to a mariner. I can give you an *exact* idea, not a rough idea. Captain Lars and I calculated that it will take us 8 days to get to the wormhole, after which we set a course for home. We'll top off our fuel tanks at one of the Azores islands. Add on another 12 days to get back to New York, which means 20 days of sailing, beginning as soon as we've moved our stuff aboard. I don't know about you, but I'm looking forward to some luxury cruise ship food. If that isn't incentive to move quickly I don't know what is."

After the meeting, Meg grabbed my hand. She didn't look happy.

"Harry, I'm really worried about something, and I haven't a clue what to do about it."

"We're going home, babe. We'll start a new life together in an already existing civilization, not a forest full of nasty animals. Why aren't you smiling?"

"I'm not concerned about you and me, Harry. You're right, we'll start our lives anew and that sounds wonderful. But I'm worried about a lot of our people, people who've become our friends, our families. I see it in a lot of faces, faces that look worried. To all of us, we've been gone for 10 years. People have moved on and started new lives in Malta Town. They all assumed that their spouses or lovers also started new lives and that they'd never see them again. So, they decided to start over again. Of the 1010 people we started out with, I counted 120 who paired off and got married, just like us. But unlike us, most of them had spouses on the other side of the friggin wormhole. You and I were single, Harry. Big difference. So, when we return to 2017, after having been gone for only two months, I can picture a bunch of husbands and wives, not to mention kids, standing on the dock to welcome back their families from the *Maltese Incident*, not realizing that in our alternate reality we've been gone for 10 years. Harry, can you picture it? 'Hi honey, great to see you. I'd like to introduce my new wife.' And I'm not even thinking about the legal details. I guess I'm being stupid, thinking about things I can't control. I hate the idea of returning our friends to emotional hell. What do you think we should do?"

"I've thought about the same issues, Meg. How's this for a plan that's been kicking around in my mind? I met a man on the *Melody* this morning, an Episcopal priest named Father Rick Sampson who's on the cruise with his wife. He's acting as the ship's chaplain. Lars told me that Father Rick is just the man to see. So, my thinking is this: first we tell the truth. Bullshit won't work. The truth, if told with care, can help make the pain go away for these folks, as well as their families. After we go through the wormhole it will take 12 days to get back to New York. During that time I suggest a series of lectures or sermons by Father Rick, addressing the problems we've been talking about. And this should be coordinated with people back in New York. While we're en route, someone needs to explain to the waiting families that we've all experienced 10 years away. Nobody can make suggestions to the families, but telling the truth will pave the way. Some people will understand that their spouses began new lives. Some won't. And here's another kicker. We've been told that the authorities have given up on the *Maltese*. We were only gone for two months in 2017 time, but those two months can be a long time if you think your spouse is dead. So, it's possible that some of the waiting families weren't waiting anymore, and went ahead with new partner arrangements themselves. All you and I can do is make sure the truth gets told, and let the new reality sink in."

"Let's make it happen, Harry."

"Oh, on the subject of priests," I said." how about we ask Father Rick to preside over our second set of wedding vows when we get back. I understand that he's the pastor of a parish on Long Island. I know my parents will freak out, and I hope your folks approve of me."

"Perfect thinking, honey. Imagine a big wedding where we won't need to post lookouts to watch for dinosaurs."

CHAPTER TWENTY-NINE

"Ali, have you prepared the report for brother Mahmood?" Amir Muhammed asked his subordinate, Ali Moradi. The two men sat in a small café in Sanaa,Yemen.

"Yes, Amir. The result of our two tests is perfection."

"There is no such thing as perfection, Ali, unless it is the personal work of Allah. But our efforts, and the brilliance of our inventor Mahmood Khan will bring glory to his holy name. Please give me a summary of our two tests to date."

"Our first test, Sheik Amir, has become known worldwide as the *Maltese Incident.* The ship held over 1,000 passengers and crew, and was laden with infidel greed. Our *Sacred Portal,* which the infidels call a 'wormhole,' is located in the archipelago known as the Azores, off the coast of Portugal."

"And how did we get the details that you are giving me, Ali?"

"One of our brothers, Raman Abdul, is a passenger on the *Maltese.* He goes by the name Jason Thomas. We arranged for him to be employed as a computer programmer for Malta Investments and also arranged for him to be a passenger on the ship."

"But wait, I'm confused about something. How can we communicate with brother Abdul if he's in another era of time?"

"He sends us messages from a small instrument that looks like a cell phone. Mahmood Khan, the genius, invented the instrument. It can communicate not just across miles but across many millennia. Brother Abdul advises us that the *Maltese* infidels erected a housing community on the land and named it named Malta Town. They even figured out a way to protect themselves from prehistoric dinosaurs."

"How long have they been gone from the present day, Ali?"

"For only two months in the present time, but 10 years in their perceived time in the past. Sheik Khan has managed to confuse the infidel with his time travel invention."

"And what about the other test, Ali? You said that it was also successful."

"Brother Mahmood placed the *Sacred Portal* in only one place in the ocean, and lured another ship to cross it. The vessel is called *Melody of the Seas*, and it carries about a thousand passengers. The captain of the ship tempted fate and lost by steaming too close to the portal. One of the passengers was a Portuguese man named Alfonso Avila, who had spent most of his life in the United States. Avila reported that he actually saw the *Maltese* disappear. Then *he* disappeared, along with everyone on the *Melody*."

"And did the *Melody* make contact with the people who were on the *Maltese*, the people who built the place called Malta Town?" Amir asked.

"Yes, Amir. According to our insider, Jason Thomas, the *Melody* has taken on all the people from Malta Town. As we speak, the ship is headed toward the *Sacred Portal*. One of the infidels is a scientist who knows about the secrets of traveling through time. Their objective is to cross our *Sacred Portal*, which they call a wormhole, and return to the present day. Of course, none of those people are aware of the instrument that Brother Thomas uses to communicate across time."

"We didn't know exactly what would happen with our first two tests, Ali, but things are working beautifully for the glory of Allah. The infidels are unaware. They think they've made a breakthrough, but we left them to flounder in ignorance."

"But, Sheik Amir, are you not concerned about the man named Bob Flowers, the scientist who has identified the idea of the *Sacred Portal*? Because he has isolated the concept, he will be able to examine the portal in detail. He will be able to unlock its secrets and share them with the infidel world."

"I will discuss the matter with Sheik Mahmood," Amir said. "According to what you told me, it will be eight days before the *Melody of the Seas* reaches the *Sacred Portal*. Brother Khan will advise me what is to become of the scientist Bob Flowers."

CHAPTER-THIRTY

"Good afternoon, ladies and gentlemen, Shannon Bream reporting for *Fox News*. The story of the two missing ships, the *Maltese* and the *Melody of the Seas* has gone from a mystery to a period of mourning. It's been two months since the *Maltese* went missing, and the *Melody of the Seas* has been gone for six hours. Most professionals involved in these matters have given up hope of ever finding the two ships. Again, I remind you that search efforts found no trace of either ship —no debris, no metallic pinging, no hope. The ships vanished, and we're left to ponder what to do about sea travel in the future.

"Although we hate to broadcast rumors, stories are circulating about whether the missing ship incidents could have been cause by an intentional act. We bring you now to the White House, where President Blake is about to make an announcement."

"Good afternoon my fellow Americans," President Blake said. "It's an understatement to say that our hearts and prayers are with the crews and passengers of the two American cruise ships that have disappeared with no trace. The government considers these incidents to be of the highest national priority. Nobody has come up with an explanation of what occurred because nobody knows just what happened to the ships. I can't address the rampant speculation that the ships' disappearance may have been caused by some group. Let me just say that nothing is off the table as we look for answers to a mystery. May God bless you, and may God bless America."

'Shannon Bream back for *Fox News*. You just heard the president. He said that the possibility of an intentional act is not off the table—nothing is. *Fox* has contacted the office of the Chairman of the Joint Chiefs of Staff, the Director of the CIA, the Director of the FBI, the office of the Chief of Naval Operations, and the Commandant of the Coast Guard. Nobody gave any indication of a lead to anybody involved in the disappearance of the two American Ships, assuming some bad actors *were* involved. So, we're either hot on somebody's tail, or we wish we were. As of now we don't know who was involved, or *if* anybody was involved. Frankly, folks, I think it's the latter—we don't know if any human being had anything to do with the disappearance of the ships. Until we uncover something more solid to tell you, this reporter still considers it a mystery."

CHAPTER THIRTY-ONE

"Anchor room, this is Captain Ragnarssen. Prepare to weigh anchor."

"Anchor is prepared to weigh sir."

"Weigh anchor."

The captain then sounded the *Melody's* horn, as the ship's band struck up *Show Me the Way To Go Home*.

A half-dozen *Pterodactyls* took flight from behind a stand of trees.

"You managed to scare the shit out of a few hundred dinosaurs, Lars," I said, as I stood next to him on the bridge.

"Not as much as they scare me, Harry. So, we're on our way. I appreciate the efficiency of your folks in moving aboard the *Melody*."

"I wish I could take credit for our speedy move, Lars, but I think everybody's desire to go wormhole hunting moved them along fast."

Bob Flowers joined us on the bridge.

"I'm sure you mariners figured this out already," Bob Flowers said, "but how can we find the coordinates of the wormhole without satellite or celestial navigation?"

"No problem, Bob," Lars said. "Like most modern cruise ships, the *Melody* carries an excellent inertial navigation system. It plots our course exactly and then enables us to backtrack to a point we crossed before. The instrument even accounts for wind, waves, and current."

"I'm going to make an announcement, Harry, and then I think you should say a word or two."

***

"Good morning, ladies and gentlemen," Ragnarssen said. "It's my honor to welcome aboard all of our guests from Malta Town. We've calculated that it will take us eight days to get to the place that Dr. Flowers calls a wormhole. If his science is correct, we'll go through the same experience we had a couple of weeks ago, and after it ends, we should find ourselves in real time, whatever real time is. You will find a few more luxuries than you experienced in Malta Town, so please enjoy our hospitality. I'm now giving the microphone to my friend, Captain Harry Fenton, who will say a few words."

"Good morning everybody, Captain Harry here. You folks from Malta Town not only elected me as mayor, but you gave me sole decision-making power before we left. I now relinquish that power in favor of Captain Lars Ragnarssen. I thank you for your assistance in helping us aboard, captain. I hope you don't find us too primitive, but we've been living among man-eating dinosaurs for the past 10 years. My colleague, Dr. Bob Flowers is the smartest human being I ever met, and I know some smart ones. Bob's a scientist as I'm sure you've heard, and he's come up with a theory that he's convinced will work. We going to pass over that same location in the ocean, a spot that Bob calls a wormhole, and that should bring us all back to the world we left. Because time flies on the other side of a wormhole, according to Bob, all of us from Malta Town are 10 years older. We've aged quite a bit, and we're looking forward to going backwards. My guess is that you folks from the *Melody* will have been gone for only a matter of hours. It will take some getting used to, although in reality we've only been gone for a bit more than two months. I spoke to the *Melody*'s chaplain, Father Rick Sampson, and he will be holding a series of meetings to help you sort out your family situations, which may have changed dramatically since we've been gone. That's all for now. If you see me wandering around the ship, just call me Harry. Enjoy your cruise."

***

"Hey, Harry, I think an interesting problem may be brewing," Meg said, as we sat and drank coffee on the balcony of our stateroom. "I notice that your friend Captain Lars is quite the ladies' man."

"That he is, hon. Lars has a well-earned reputation as a skirt chaser. Is there a problem?"

"He's been flirting like crazy with Sandy Jones, Bob and Mary Jones' daughter."

"So, what's the problem, Madam Schoolmom? Isn't Sandy in her early 20s?"

"She's 21 to be exact, Harry. In a few days, if Bob's theory holds out, she'll be 11 years old."

"Oh shit," I said. "Lars will need to stop thinking with his dick. Don't worry, hon, I'll talk to him."

***

"Harry, it's Lars," said the captain over our stateroom phone. "Would you and Meg please join me for lunch along with a few others? I also invited Al Avila, who used to be with Naval Intelligence when he lived in the States, along with a fellow known as Buster, who is some kind of government investigator. Bob Flowers will join us as well."

"Will Sandy Jones be with us?" I asked.

"No," Lars said. "Should I invite her?"

"No, I wouldn't do that," I said. "Let's you and I have a chat after lunch."

We gathered for lunch in the captain's dining room overlooking the ocean.

"Good afternoon, everybody," Lars said. "Not that I need an excuse to dine with charming people, but I've convened this lunch at the request of our friend, Doctor Bob Flowers. I'll turn our meeting over to Bob as soon as the waiter takes our orders."

Franz the waiter came to our table. "Good afternoon, ladies and gentlemen. Today's specials are a choice of three delicious fish offerings, made to perfection by our chef."

Meg, Dr. Bob, and I, the three former residents of Malta Town, shook our heads.

"Do you have beef, chicken, rat, anything but fish?" I asked.

The three of us ordered filet mignon. We also skipped the smoked trout appetizer, opting instead for potato leek soup.

"Hi everybody," said Dr. Bob after lunch and small talk. "As you all know I tend to sit still and stare a lot. Don't worry. It's just me tapping into my brain. So here we are on the final leg of a strange journey. We all hope it's the final leg. So, what are we left with? All of us are curious people, not just those of us who look for clues for a living. Suppose we go through the wormhole and everything works as I predict. We will come out the other end in a different time, and we'll all live happily ever after. But if you're like me, that isn't the end of it. We still would like to know how this happened to us. Here's a question for Buster. How did the federal government get involved in this?"

"Bob, let me put it bluntly. I'm aboard this ship on direct orders from the White House. Somebody upstairs wants to know what's going on, and so do I. Two ships go missing and one of them finds its way back by travelling across the same spot in the ocean. How did that happen? I don't mean that as a scientific question. If your theory is correct, Bob, and it sure sounds logical, we'll know how that happened. But was it just a coincidence? Here's my big question—was somebody involved in making these two events occur? Was there a bad actor or actors who started things moving. In other words, who put the wormhole there? If anybody else wants to know the answer to that question, please raise your hand."

Everyone at the table raised their hands, except for Dr. Bob.

"I notice that you didn't raise your hand, Bob."

"Buster, as an occasional poker player, I agree with you completely, but as a scientist I can't rule out the element of chance. After all, it's a small spot in the ocean. If you're trying to see if some human actor put the wormhole there—and I don't know how that could be possible—I'm willing to help you find the answer to your question."

The ship took a gentle lurch, as if it collided with a large wave. But the sea was calm.

Everybody stood and looked out the window. A *Megalodon* passed gracefully by the *Melody*. A rifleman stationed on that side of the ship opened fire, and the giant fish swam rapidly away.

***

Meg and I walked around the deck after lunch. Neither of us had anything pressing to do, and we agreed that it felt strange.

"Hey, captain, do you feel odd not having to make decisions and answer questions all the time?"

"I can't believe that I'm a passenger on a ship. Yes, it feels strange and good at the same time. How about you? You look more relaxed than I've seen you in a long while."

"I do feel relaxed, but something's been bothering me. What about us, Harry? What big changes will we face? I don't have a clue, and neither do you. We didn't build Malta Town by sitting around thinking what will be next. We made our own future, just like you and I are about to do again. All I know is I love you more than my own life, and our lives are about to restart. I want to hear a positive idea right now from your handsome face."

"How's this?" I said. "That crazy wormhole event brought us together. If it means being with you, I'd go through the whole thing again."

"Not that I want to change the subject, but what do you think about that guy Buster's idea that somebody may be responsible for all this crap. What do you think?"

"If somebody somehow put that wormhole there, I think the government isn't going to let up until it finds out who. And how."

CHAPTER THIRTY-TWO

"Sheik Khan, the ship *Melody of the Seas* is approaching the *Sacred Portal.* They should cross it in five hours," Ali Muhammed said to Sheik Mahmood Khan, the inventor.

"Did you learn this from Brother Raman Abdul, our spy on the *Melody* who goes by the infidel name Jason Thomas?"

"Yes, sir. If I may say so, the man is invaluable," Ali said.

"I have been working with the targeting satellite. As of now, my plan is to leave the *Sacred Portal* exactly where it is."

"Do I understand you correctly that you can program the satellite to place *Sacred Portals* wherever you wish?"

"You understand perfectly, young Ali. Allah has given me the power to rain confusion on the infidels at will. Right now, Dr. Flowers has convinced people that there is but one *Sacred Portal,* and all they need to do is cross over the exact position to get back to the present. Soon, the infidel will be afraid to go to sea in any ship."

"Is it only in the ocean that you can place a *Sacred Portal*, Sheik Khan?" Asked Ali.

"Oh no, my young friend. Allah has given me the power, through our satellite, to place a portal anywhere on earth." He cracked up laughing again. Soon, the infidel will be afraid to leave his house for fear of being transported to another time. The caliphate will rule from a satellite in space. When we wish the infidel to do our bidding, he will not dare to refuse. If we desire that all women have their heads and faces covered, all we need to do is command it. Collecting the *Jizya*, or tax, on the non-believers, will become a simple matter of demanding that it be turned over. All the vast multitudes of infidels will be *dhimmis,* subjects living in our lands. The glorious caliphate will rule forever. Whenever the unbelievers displease us, we will simply send them to another time."

"One thing you never told me, Sheik Mahmood, is how were able to put the satellite into space, and how did we manufacture the elements necessary for it to create *Sacred Portals?*"

"A man of great wealth named Joseph Morgan. He keeps himself so secret that he did not choose a Muslim name when he converted. He uses his vast riches for the furtherance of Islam and the subjugation of the infidel. Allah has blessed me with a fertile mind, a mind capable of creating wonderful science. But it is Joseph Morgan and his money that have enabled us to achieve what we've done. He and his aerospace company are working on plans to launch many more satellites so that we can lay down a *Sacred Portal* at a moment's notice anywhere on earth."

"What of the American scientist Bob Flowers, Sheik Mahmood? Did you not say that you had a plan for Brother Abdul to question him while they are on the ship?"

"I have given Brother Abdul a list of questions to ask Dr. Flowers. Our goal is to find out how much he knows. I gave Brother Abdul instructions to take care of Dr. Flowers before they cross the *Sacred Portal.*"

"Take care of him?"

"Yes, Ali. Kill him."

CHAPTER THIRTY-THREE

"What's wrong with a guy who suddenly develops a personality, Meg?"

"It's something out of the ordinary, Harry, way out of the ordinary. That guy, Jason Thomas, is positively weird. That's not just my opinion. Ask around. Dr. Theresa refused to work with him because she thinks he's a creep. People tell me that Thomas has always been quiet and never social, and they've been observing this bird for 10 years. Suddenly, he's Mr. Friendly, and not just with anybody. It seems he's become a big fan of Bob Flowers. He follows Bob wherever he goes, and constantly asks questions. Bob himself thought it was a bit weird. It seems that Thomas wants to know everything that Bob knows about the wormhole."

"So, Bob is a whiz of a scientist," I said. "It's natural that he'd acquire a fan club. You're becoming too much of a cynic, hon. But I agree, Thomas is a weird one."

"Harry, does it bother you that such an odd bird is trailing Bob Flowers and asking him constant questions?"

"It does bother me a bit, now that you raise the question. Bob Flowers is the most important person on this ship, for obvious reasons. He's the time travel maven. What else have you noticed about the mysterious Jason Thomas?"

"We spent 10 years with 1,000 people, first at sea, then in a community ashore," Meg said. "Some of the people were delightful, some not. But the weirdest one of all is Jason Thomas. He is a total creep. In 10 years he hardly spoke to me, except that time when he said that all the women should wear scarves."

Meg and I walked to the bridge to talk to Captain Lars. Bob Flowers was already there. Jason Thomas had requested permission to enter the bridge, apparently to be near Bob Flowers. Captain Lars declined his request, explaining that the bridge was getting too crowded with non-essential personnel.

"I need a nap," Bob Flowers said. "When my brain is in overdrive, I need to take a rest. About a half-hour should do the trick."

He had just left the bridge when Meg noticed that he was tailed by Jason Thomas. Buster had just joined us on the bridge.

"Hey, look." Meg yelled to Buster and me. "Mystery man is on the heels of our friend Bob."

Buster took out his pistol and chambered a round. I did the same, and so did Meg. The last thing any of us would tolerate is somebody lifting a finger against Bob Flowers, our key to the wormhole.

We ran to the elevator to take it below to Bob Flowers' room. We pounded on his door, which he opened to let us in.

"Can't a man take a nap?" Flowers said.

Have you seen that guy Jason Thomas?" Buster asked. "We saw him following you."

The door swung open and Jason Thomas ran in with his gun drawn. He opened fire, the bullet hitting the television. Meg fired two rounds at the man's midsection. Seconds later, Thomas lay dead.

Buster retrieved a room key from Thomas' pocket. We searched his room and found a trove of radical literature and photographs of Thomas in Arab robes.

"Hey, look at this." I held up a piece of paper showing latitude and longitude. Above the coordinates were words in Arabic.

Buster looked at the words and said, "It means *Sacred Portal*. The words on the bottom of the paper read, 'page 24.' Obviously, it's from a book.

I called Lars on the bridge.

"Lars, Jason Thomas is dead. He pulled a gun on us and Meg took him out. Please check out this position." I read the coordinates.

"That's the wormhole, Harry. Where are you reading that from?" Lars said.

"A piece of paper we found in Thomas' room," I said. "The inscription above the coordinates is the words *Sacred Portal,* in Arabic. Buster translated it."

We searched the room for every book we could find and looked at page 24.

"Here it is," Buster said. "Lure the infidel to the *Sacred Portal,* where he will be lost in time and space, never to return unless he finds the spot where the *Sacred Portal* was located."

"What impact does this have on our immediate plans, Bob?" Captain Lars asked.

"The words seem to support my theory. I have absolutely no idea how anyone could create a wormhole. I recommend that we keep heading for the wormhole and hope that we don't hit another one on the way."

***

Meg was suddenly quiet, rare for her.

"Hey, what's wrong, hon? You're never this quiet," I said.

"I never killed anybody before," Meg said. "I never even aimed a gun somebody. My dad taught me to how to shoot, but only for target practice. Shooting dinosaurs didn't bother me, but killing Jason Thomas was different. He was a human being, not a good human being, but still, he was a living, breathing person. I can't get his face out of my mind when I shot him. I don't think I'll ever get it out of my mind."

"Meg, Jason Thomas jumped at us and opened fire. He was looking to kill people, including you and me. When I was in the Navy I took a lot of lives, and even though I was in combat, it bothered me. That's right, it bothered me to shoot live ammo at another human being. It may surprise you to know that it upset me, but it did. What you're feeling is normal, babe. So, listen to your captain. Maybe say a prayer for the guy, but right now I want you to give me a hug."

Meg broke down in tears, which I thought was a good thing. Let it all out, get in touch with your feelings and do all the stuff psychologists tell us to do.

***

"Brother Raman doesn't reply." Ali said. "He told us that he was going to take care of Dr. Flowers. Maybe Raman was apprehended."

"Anything is possible, Ali," Amir Moradi said. "I spoke to Sheik Khan who has decided he will let the Americans proceed to the *Sacred Portal*. He will deal with them after they return to 2017. Sheik Khan is concerned about using the satellite too much, for fear that it may be discovered by electronic surveillance. The infidels think that they are about to return home. Soon, they will wish they were still among the dinosaurs."

CHAPTER THIRTY-FOUR

"Captain, we're a half-hour to the coordinates," the first officer said. "You told me to remind you so you could make an announcement."

"Good afternoon, everyone, this is Captain Ragnarssen on the bridge. We're on track, heading to the location of the wormhole that will take us home. We're 30 minutes from the coordinates. I will announce a countdown as we approach the position. It's daylight, so we can expect that we'll cruise into darkness and then emerge into daylight again— daylight in 2017."

"Lars, I'm concerned about something," I said. "When we show up on the other side of the wormhole, do you expect that the area will be crowded with ships and boats looking for us?"

"Good point, Harry. It's great to have another captain to look over my shoulder. I think we'll just need to take our chances. My guess is that the search operation has been pared back because we've been gone so long. But you make an excellent point. I'll remind the passengers of that possibility."

"Five minutes to the position, captain," the first officer said.

"This is Captain Ragnarssen again, ladies and gentlemen. We're five minutes from our target. Please be prepared for extreme sea conditions. We don't know if we're going to encounter other vessels when we emerge from the wormhole, but please be prepared for turbulence. The countdown will commence shortly."

"Read me the countdown when we hit 10 seconds, Bob."

"Zero minus ten, nine, eight…We're on the target, captain."

The daylight turned dark, and the ship began to rumble. Two minutes went by, and daylight returned, much brighter than before. The rumbling stopped.

"Right full rudder," Captain Lars screamed at the top of his voice.

A Coast Guard cutter steamed off our port side, no more than 200 feet from us. The two ships passed by each other, avoiding a collision by no more than 50 feet. Lars looked at me.

"I think you Navy types have a phrase for what almost happened, Harry."

"Yeah, a collision at sea will ruin your day."

The bridge was strangely silent. The thrill of emerging from the wormhole was dampened by our near collision with the cutter. When we saw that we were safe, everyone on the bridge joined the entire ship in yelling and cheering.

"Hey, Slim, where did your gray hair go?" Meg said as she ran her fingers through my hair. I wrapped my arms around her.

"You look as beautiful now as you did millions of years ago." I pinched her cute ass, her now-little ass.

Bob Flowers broke into a tap dance, his arthritic hip pain-free.

"*Melody of the Seas*, this is Captain Duane Peterson of the US Coast Guard Cutter *Endurance*, come in please."

"This is Captain Lars Ragnarssen of the *Melody of the Seas*. Read you loud and clear, Captain Peterson. Thank God we missed each other."

"Where the hell did you guys come from?" Peterson said.

"It's a long story, captain, as long as 10 years. I'm happy to say you can stop looking for us. The *Maltese* isn't with us, but all her passengers and crew are aboard the *Melody*, so you can stop looking for her as well. We're setting our course for New York Harbor. Will you provide escort service for us?"

"I don't have enough fuel for that trip, captain, but the American destroyer, *Forrest Sherman* is approaching your position. Her commanding officer, Captain Langdon, will be talking to you."

"Harry, isn't Langdon the man who wrote the book about you?" Meg asked.

"Yes, that's him, hon. I'm glad he'll be escorting us. He's a good man and a good sailor."

"*Melody of the Seas*, this is *Forrest Sherman*, Captain James Langdon speaking. Is that you, Lars?"

"Hello, Jim. Great to hear your voice. I guess you've been wondering where we've been. We've been wondering the same thing. We're not the only ones on this trip, but have about 1,000 new guests aboard, the passengers and crew of none other than the *Maltese*. A guy named Harry Fenton is next to me, and he wants to say hello."

"Hi Jim, Harry Fenton here. It's good to know that a solid tin-can sailor is running interference for us. I look forward to seeing you in New York."

"Harry, I cannot fucking believe that I'm talking to you," Langdon said. "I'm jotting down notes for the next edition of *The Harry Fenton Story*."

"This is Lars again, Jim. A passenger from the federal government tells me that we're going to spend a lot of time being questioned by the FBI. I'm sure they'll want to talk to you too. A lot of people are more than mildly curious to know what happened to the *Maltese* and the *Melody*."

Lars announced an immediate meeting in the main theater. People could barely hear him above the pandemonium. Lars asked Meg and me to join him on the dais. As we entered the theater, 11-year-old Sandy Jones passed by and said, "Hi, Captain Lars."

"Cute kid," Lars said. "She looks familiar."

Meg and I cracked up. "She's the 21-year-old babe you were flirting with a few of days ago, Lars," Meg said.

Lars shook his head and laughed.

***

The *Melody* entered New York Harbor at 11 a.m. on Saturday July 15, 2017 and headed for its slip at Pier 88 on the West Side of Manhattan. It seemed that half of New York City turned out. Fire boats gushed streams of water from their hose nozzles and confetti coated the city. The Mayor of New York City was there to give Captain Lars and me the keys to the city. President Blake called to speak to us on the *Melody*'s bridge and invited us to the White House.

"So, we're off to see the FBI, Honey," Meg said.

"After living among *Velociraptors,* I'm ready for anything."

CHAPTER THIRTY-FIVE

Sarah Watson, Director of the FBI, called a meeting at the FBI New York office at 26 Federal Plaza. She invited a select group of people connected to the *Maltese* and *Melody* incidents. In attendance would be Captain Lars, Dr. Bob Flowers, Randy Borg, Buster of course, Meg, and me. Although Watson had no jurisdiction over him, Al Avila agreed to attend. Norwegian Cruise Line sent two limos to the ship to bring us all downtown.

Before the meeting began, Watson called Buster to the side.

"I can't believe what I'm about to tell you, Buster, but we have strong evidence that a person or a group was directly involved in both incidents. Your experience was incredible enough, but this adds a layer of criminality to the mystery. I can't mention it at the meeting, and you are to keep it under wraps. We need to lure this conspiracy into the open so we can kill it."

"But Sarah, how the hell could somebody create a wormhole in the ocean and take hundreds of people back in time?"

"That's what we need to find out," Watson said. "The good news is that we've got people on the inside. This is obviously top secret, of course. Captain Harry Fenton will work with you because we need somebody with a maritime background. I also want Meg Fenton, Harry's wife, to work on the case. I've heard that she's smart as hell and the two of them are inseparable. Buster, we're counting on you. You're an engineer who speaks fluent Arabic and you have the ingenuity of a hungry rat. If anybody can break this thing open, it's you."

"I'll take your reference to me as a hungry rat under advisement, Madam Director," Buster said, laughing.

"Okay, it's time for the meeting." Watson said.

***

"Good morning everyone, and thank you for being here, even without a subpoena."

FBI humor. We all laughed politely.

Meg and I walked up to the front of the room and handed Watson a wrapped gift. She opened it and cracked up laughing. It was a photo of Meg and me, rifles in one hand, and flashing a thumbs-up with the other. We each stood with one foot on the head of a dead *Velociraptor*.

"I'll cherish this always," Watson said. "I know just the place to hang it. Although you meant it as a joke, it really serves to illustrate one of the things we'll discuss this morning—the ordeal you folks went through, dinosaurs and all. Let me say that neither the CIA nor the FBI considers this case closed. Before I go on, I want to acknowledge Captain Harry Fenton. My husband was a destroyer sailor and gave me a book to read about Harry. It's an honor to have a man with your courage working with us. Whether it's Iranian gunboats or dinosaurs, you're a tough guy."

The meeting went on for another two hours. Sarah Watson concentrated mainly on the experience of travelling through a wormhole.

"When I was a young agent," Watson said, "I once got lost in a forest. As frightening as that was, it can't compare to what you folks went through. We'll take a short break."

Meg leaned over and whispered in my ear.

"Harry, Sarah Watson used the words 'working with us.' What the hell does that mean?"

I really didn't know what she meant. I'd find out soon enough.

CHAPTER THIRTY-SIX

The crew of the Royal Caribbean cruise ship *Ocean Magic* prepared to get underway from its homeport, known as Port Liberty, in Bayonne, New Jersey. Although the *Ocean Magic* had a capacity of 3,000 passengers, the ship would put to sea light, with only 900 passengers aboard and a crew of 250. The serious drop-off in bookings because of the *Maltese* and *Melody* incidents was the talk of the cruise ship industry. Although the missing ship incidents had happy endings, the public was still skittish about going to sea.

The return of the *Melody of the Seas*, along with the passengers and crew of the *Maltese,* was met with nationwide jubilation. The good cheer, however, did not result in an increase in bookings. Cruise ship companies were growing accustomed to offering deep discounts to lure travelers to sea, and struggled to create a happy cruise experience with a skeleton crew.

Management of the cruise ship companies realized that they didn't just compete against each other, but against a phenomenon that nobody understood. The two near-disasters had happy endings, but nobody knew why, and nobody knew how to prevent the next ship from disappearing. Competing against the unknown is something that would take some getting used to. The cruise lines began a massive public relations campaign to get people to start booking cruises again. A divorce attorney with a morbid sense of humor took out an ad that read: "Show your ex-spouse that you care. Book her on a cruise."

***

"Good afternoon, ladies and gentlemen, this is Martha MacCallum for *Fox News.*

We welcome as our guest in the Fox Studio, Mr. Jeremy Escondido, a vice president with Viking Cruise Line, a company that has seen a 90 percent drop in bookings, just like all cruise ship companies. Jeremy, please convince me and our audience that we should book a cruise for our next vacation."

"Martha, it's no secret why people are wary about cruising these days. The strange events that happened to the *Maltese* and the *Melody of the Seas* caught everyone's imagination. But there's a happy ending. Everybody is home safe and sound. What looked like disasters turned out to be fascinating adventures."

"Adventures?" MacCallum gasped, her face appearing stunned. "The ship *Maltese* is still missing, although its crew and passengers have been rescued. And I remind you that there's no official explanation yet as to what exactly happened to either the *Maltese* or *the Melody of the Seas*."

"Martha, I think it's important to note that both disappearances occurred in the Azores, and both near a certain position in the ocean. Bulletins have gone out to all shipping companies, cruise ship lines, national coast guards and navies, to beware of that section of the ocean in the Azores. It's a shame that people are giving up wonderful vacation experiences because of a strange anomaly in one small area of the vast ocean."

"Jeremy, thank you for coming on our show. So, folks, it's your choice; avoid the Azores—or avoid cruising altogether."

CHAPTER THIRTY-SEVEN

Dereck Burton, Captain of the *Ocean Magic*, ordered the ship's horn to sound as she cast off her lines from the dock at Port Liberty in Bayonne, New Jersey. She sailed into a warm, calm July night. As the ship glided under the Verrazano-Narrows Bridge, Captain Burton ordered the first officer to sound the horn again, although the Rules of the Road didn't call for, or even sanction such a tactic. Burton didn't care. If the Coast Guard questioned him about it, he would say that he did it to alert harbor traffic. The real reason he sounded the horn was to call attention to the ship as she sailed under the bridge, because he wanted to do everything he could to promote cruising vacations. He hated that people avoided cruising because of a couple of strange event thousands of miles away. He hated it, but he couldn't blame them. Whenever he thought about the *Maltese* or the *Melody of the Seas*, he forced the ideas from his head. The reason he forced the thoughts from his head was because he didn't *want* to think about it. He had passengers—and a career—to be concerned about.

He looked forward to a short, pleasant cruise. The ship would spend the next two days at sea, and then put into Hamilton, Bermuda. Following cruise ship custom, the captain would dine with a different group of people each night. Burton anticipated the conversations—the same conversations. People would want to know everything about his thoughts on the *Maltese* and *Melody* incidents. He would explain to the passengers, as he explained to anybody who would listen, that those two events were oddballs and they both occurred in the same small area of the ocean, far away in the Azores. There was nothing to worry about when taking a sea cruise. He always emphasized that people shouldn't worry about something that wouldn't happen and spoil their vacation.

But Burton was lying, and he knew it. He did enough worrying for everybody. He listened to the executives from the home office making their rounds on TV shows, telling everybody what he told his passengers—there's nothing to worry about. But why, Burton wondered, hasn't any scientist come forward with an explanation of just what the hell happened? That's the missing element in all the public relations efforts— simply tell the truth or admit that you don't know the truth. And even though he did his best to join in the cruise industry public relations campaign, he knew that he really didn't have any answers.

Burton stepped outside onto the open bridge after telling Peter Dugan, his first officer, to take over. He lit a cigarette, which always relaxed him when something was on his mind. The ship traveled at 18 knots with a trailing wind of the same speed. It made for a comfortable smoke without ashes flying all over the place. The sky was beautiful, with sparkling stars and a three-quarter moon.

Burton's heart skipped a beat when he thought he saw a plane heading straight for the bridge, its bright lights bathing the area in sudden illumination. Then he realized that it wasn't a plane, but a sky full of daylight. He unconsciously dropped his cigarette into his shirt pocket, where it began to smolder. He beat his hand against the pocket and ran inside to get some water. As he reached for a water bottle he felt the ship begin to rumble. He looked at Dugan.

"Dear God," Dugan said, "this is what those other ships went through."

But they weren't in the Azores. They were 50 miles off the coast of New Jersey. The daylight returned to darkness, pitch darkness. They could no longer see the stars. The moon was no longer three-quarters but had disappeared.

"Captain, do you think you should make an announcement?" Dugan asked.

"And tell them what? That all those times I said not to worry I was lying?"

He picked up the microphone.

"We've experienced a strange weather event, ladies and gentlemen. I'll provide you with more information in the morning."

Dugan looked at him and said nothing.

"How'd I do Peter? Do you think I put their fears to rest? Be honest with me."

"I'll be perfectly honest with you, captain. I wouldn't be surprised if we confront an angry mob shortly. You told them nothing, and that means they'll fill in the blanks by themselves. These passengers read newspapers and watch TV just like everybody. I'm sure most of them read all about the *Maltese* and the *Melody* incidents. In the morning you'll need to go through with your promise to provide more information."

***

Morning came for the crew and passengers of the *Ocean Magic*. No clouds were visible in the sky, but the day was gray and bleak and totally overcast.

"Our navigational instruments are shot to shit, captain. Last night you turned the ship around to head back to New York. We should be there by now, but there's nothing but wide-open ocean around us. Our compass heading says that we're head west, but the mainland is nowhere in sight. Even our inertial navigation system isn't working. We've sent out a *mayday*, but nobody answers. We have no idea where we are.

Dugan convinced Captain Burton that he should deliver a detailed announcement to the crew and passengers. His brief address right after the event just wouldn't do, and probably made things worse. Nothing gets people angrier than being lied to.

"Be honest with them captain. I suggest that you tell them what we know about the *Maltese* and *Melody* events, and describe the similarities."

"But to be honest with them I would need to say that I haven't the foggiest fucking idea what happened."

"So, tell them that, Captain. Just leave out the f-bomb."

"Ladies and gentlemen, this is Captain Burton. Last night, we experienced a strange phenomenon—strange to say the least. We've all read about the experience of the ships *Maltese* and *Melody of the Seas*. Those two incidents occurred over a thousand miles from here in the Azores, off the coast of Portugal. Well, here we are steaming off New Jersey, and it appears that we've encountered a similar event. Because we're in American waters, we expect that assistance from the Coast Guard is on its way."

He looked at Dugan.

"The event occurred over eight hours ago, so where the hell is the Coast Guard?" Dugan whispered. "Shoot straight with them, captain, or they'll panic."

"The Coast Guard often takes time to arrive on a scene because they like to be thorough," Burton said into the microphone. "Please enjoy your breakfast. I'll keep you advised throughout the day."

"I can tell from the look on your face, Pete, that you didn't find my talk impressive."

"Forget about me, captain. It's the others you need to impress. I suggest an up-date at least every couple of hours."

"Look about 10 points off the port bow," Captain Burton said, "a couple of miles from us. Have you ever seen ships like that?"

"As you know, Captain, I'm a naval history buff. Those four ships we're looking at are German men of war, about 1930s vintage. Remember from the public hearings about the *Maltese* and the *Melody*. Both of those ships found themselves millions of years in the past."

"You don't mean to fucking tell me that…"

"Yes, captain, we've traveled through time."

***

Meg and I were sipping FBI coffee in the snack room during a break.

"Honey, we're not cops," Meg said. "I think the FBI and the CIA are on top of this case and they don't need our help. And what's that bullshit about your security clearance being updated?"

"Didn't you hear Watson?" I asked. "They also ran a background check on you. Apparently, she is impressed with our teamwork. Hey, maybe we can wear those cool flak vests with 'FBI' emblazoned across the front and back."

"Don't be an asshole," Meg recommended.

"Let's catch the news while we're standing here," I said. "In Malta Town, we were always starved for news."

We looked at the TV in the corner of the snack room while we sipped our coffee.

"Good afternoon, ladies and gentlemen, Wolf Blitzer reporting for CNN. I have something shocking news that got mixed into today's happy story. Just as New York and the entire country are celebrating the safe return of the people from the *Maltese* and *Melody Incidents,* we're hit with yet another maritime mystery. The Celebrity Line cruise ship, *Ocean Magic,* disappeared last night. This incident didn't happen in the Azores as did the other two events, but 50 miles off the coast of New Jersey. Just as with the previous two incidents, the ship simply disappeared. The search-and-rescue operation is just getting underway, so there's still hope that there may be survivors. The *Maltese* and *Melody Incidents* are under intense scrutiny by law enforcement and intelligence agencies as well as academic institutions, especially around the subject of time travel. At this point, we have no solid news to bring you about the *Ocean Magic,* except that it's missing. We will update you throughout the day as we hear more."

Meg looked at me. "Oh shit," we both said.

Everyone began to file back into the meeting area after the break. An agent we hadn't met stood at the front of the room. She introduced herself as Agent Pat Blackwell.

"Director Watson will be with us shortly after she gets off the phone," Blackwell said. "She's talking to the White House. I don't know if any of you heard about it during the break, but another ship has gone missing, this one off the coast of New Jersey. Same familiar stuff—no debris, no sonar return, nothing. It happened last night."

"I think the cruise ship industry has seen better times," Lars said.

"Leave it to a Scandinavian to come up with a studied understatement," I whispered to Meg.

Meg still thought the idea of working for the FBI sucked. I was inclined to agree with her.

***

"A gentleman is here to see you, Buster."

I was sitting in my temporary office at 26 Federal Plaza.

"What's his name?"

"He said you know him."

"Welcome home, Buster," CIA Director Bill Carlini said as he walked into the conference room. He wore a pulled-down hat, dark sunglasses, and an upturned collar.

"I figured I'd try looking like a spook rather than just being one. I understand that the cruise I sent you on turned out to be interesting."

Bill and I, although we're old friends, both share the same preference for getting right to the point.

"You heard the news about the ship that disappeared off New Jersey?" I said.

"I heard it on the morning news while having breakfast," Carlini said. "I almost lost what I had just eaten."

"And the craziest thing about this incident is that it didn't happen in the Azores but 50 miles from New Jersey," I said. "This shit is getting out of hand."

"As far as the CIA is concerned, it got out of hand when the first ship disappeared," Carlini said. "With most disasters there's either a feeling of hope or despair. When you people all came back safely, we thought that the weird story was over. The ship that disappeared off New Jersey puts a whole new light on all this crap. It's no longer a phenomenon of the Azores. Look at a model of the globe and ask yourself if you would feel safe in any ocean."

"Mr. Director"—I always call him Mr. Director when I want to hit him over the head with something important. "You sent me on that cruise to solve the case of the *Maltese Incident*. Well, I not only encountered the *Maltese*, but I got personally involved with the *Melody of the Seas Incident*. Sarah Watson tells me that I've got the ingenuity of a hungry rat. I used every bit of that ingenuity scurrying along the decks on my lovely cruise."

"So, my hungry rat friend, can you give me an executive summary of your findings?"

"Yes, sir, I can, and here's my summary—I don't have a goddam clue as to what happened."

"But you must know more than when you started," Carlini said.

"Well sure, but I didn't solve anything. Here's what we've learned, and it's all on the record from Sarah Watson's office over the past few days. The *Maltese*, and then the *Melody of the Seas* hit a thing called a wormhole in the Azores. A wormhole is a portal from one dimension of time to another. The people on the *Maltese* thought they had been gone for 10 years. But they were only gone for two months, local time. A scientist from the *Maltese* group named Bob Flowers figured out that to return to the present we had to cross over the same wormhole. We did, and here we are. Fascinating stuff, and you should read it. But the bottom line, Bill, is that I have not solved a fucking thing."

"Buster, we've known each other for a long time, so let me ask you a question. What are you going to do now?"

"I'm going to huddle with a guy who always seems to unblock cases for me when I'm stuck, a guy with the perception of a finely tuned radio receiver."

"You mean Imam Mike?"

"Yes, that's exactly who I mean. I have no idea how he can help, but then I never do. He has a wonderful habit of surprising me. I guess I won't get a sea cruise out of this."

"Not unless you can cruise from here to Brooklyn."

CHAPTER THIRTY-EIGHT

Meg and I went to Sarah Watson's office, as she requested. All the people from the previous meeting had left, and we would be the only ones in this meeting. When we walked through the door, Watson's aide almost ran us over to escort us to her inner office.

"I think Watson is in a hurry to see us," I said.

"I can't wait," Meg said. She didn't look happy.

When we entered Watson's office she sat at her desk with her hands folded in front of her, adopting a demeanor that announced, "I've got something heavy to lay on you."

"Harry, let me come right out and ask you something," Watson said. "Can you guess what it is?"

"Yes," I said, "I think I do." Meg nodded, as if she knew too.

"You want us to appear on *Jeopardy*," I said. Wiseasses often find it difficult to control themselves, as Meg's elbow to my arm reminded me.

Watson laughed.

"I'm guessing that you want me to try to find that ship, the *Ocean Magic,*" I said, this time shooting for seriousness.

"You hit the nail right on the head, Harry. Since the amazing experience you folks went through, we've all become educated in this thing called time travel, which I used to think was a subject for science fiction novels. Before this incident, I thought a wormhole was a hole in your lawn left by a worm."

I could tell she expected us to laugh.

We didn't.

"Do we have a reliable fix of the location where the ship disappeared?" I asked.

"Yes, we do," Sarah said. "Since the incidents involving the *Maltese* and the *Melody*, cruise ship companies keep careful satellite tracks of all their ships at sea. So, we think we've got an exact fix on where the *Ocean Magic* left us, which means we know where the wormhole is."

"Madam Director," Meg said, with a clear edge on her voice, "we'd all be crazy, not just the FBI but our whole society, if we didn't go after that ship and its people. I say that because we're all pretty sure what happened. I just hope that you're not looking to Harry to lead the charge."

Meg's not only good with a gun, she's sharp with words too.

"Yes, Meg, that's exactly what we've been thinking. And not only Harry. I know that you two are a close married couple, and from what I heard about the tales of that place called Malta Town, you're a tight-knit team in every sense. We'd like you to help Harry find the ship. So, what are your thoughts? Harry?"

Meg gave me a glance like an arrow. I squeezed her hand.

"Madam Director…"

"Please call me Sarah."

"Okay, Sarah. Without boring you with details about how Meg and I are looking forward to starting our lives over, let me point out some simple facts. Once you go through a wormhole, you're still on a vessel, and you're still in the ocean. It takes no more skill for a modern captain to run his ship on the other side of the wormhole as he does on this side. It's a ship on the water, only in a different time. We don't know where that New Jersey wormhole leads. On the *Maltese* we went back few million years, and we still don't know how the hell we did it. The point is, Meg and I have put in our time, served our time, if you will. All you need is an experienced captain and a willing crew. Their job is simple when you break it down to its essentials. Find the *Ocean Magic* and lead her back to the wormhole. Just make sure the rescue ship has plenty of fuel and aircraft or drones to search for the missing ship. Even as a consultant, there isn't a hell of a lot I can tell a captain about the job. Put me and Meg into a room with a volunteer captain, and we'll get the guy up to speed in a half hour. We don't need to tell him how to kill dinosaurs."

"Harry, I can't force you and I wouldn't want to. But you're a man with proven skill, ingenuity, and courage. Where do I find a guy like you?"

"The Navy is full of good captains, Sarah," Meg said. "Just ask Harry. He knows most of them. If I'm not out of line, I would like to offer a suggestion. Make it a volunteer operation. Plenty of people would jump at the idea, people who are brave or adventuresome or both."

"If I could take it a step further, Sarah," I said, "I would pick a nuclear-powered ship that doesn't need to stop for gas. Meg's right. You won't have a hard time finding volunteers."

"Do you two see this as a dangerous operation?" Watson asked.

"We know a hell of a lot more about wormholes now than we did just a few weeks ago," I said, "but we have to admit that there's a lot we don't know. Hell, we traveled to the time of the dinosaurs. We just don't know if it will be dangerous or not. What I do know is that I want to spend the rest of my life with this woman next to me, without looking over my shoulder for prehistoric animals."

"Harry, it was my intention today to convince you to take command of a ship to search for the *Ocean Magic* on the other side of the wormhole. I heard your words and I also heard Meg's. I don't want to give you a swelled head, but nobody can do a job like this better than Harry Fenton, assisted by his more than able wife. There are over 1,000 people on the other side of that wormhole, and we've got to find them and bring them back home."

Sarah Watson is a persuasive woman. After she said the words "we've got to find them and bring them back home," she just let the words hang in the air for a few moments. During those moments she stared at me like a nun I had in the fifth grade who had just asked me to walk my little cousin Billy home. Billy had missed his school bus. Sister Carol, my parents, and little Billy's parents, all agreed that he should be my responsibility, and I could tell that Sister Carol didn't give a rat's ass that

I wanted to play baseball after school that day. I began to feel like a real dick for trying to shirk what I knew was my responsibility.

"So, let me be as direct as I can," Watson continued. "Harry, I propose that you be reactivated to active duty status as a captain in the United States Navy, and I also propose that Meg be given a direct commission as a Navy lieutenant. I already cleared that with the Office of Naval Operations and the White House. But before either of you say anything, I want you both to go down the hallway to the bathrooms where you will find mirrors. I want you each to look into the mirror and say the following: 'I refuse to rescue those people.' After you're done please return to my office and give me the decisions that you've given yourselves."

If I don't take him, I thought, how the hell is little Billy going to get home?

Meg and I did as we were asked. We skipped the part about looking in the mirror. Instead we looked into each other's eyes, which for us is like looking into a mirror.

"Sarah's asking us to rescue a thousand people, hon," I said to Meg. "From the look in your eyes, I think I know your answer."

"Let's go wormhole hunting, captain."

We walked back into Watson's office.

"Okay, Sarah, we're in," I said.

We shook hands and agreed to meet later in the afternoon to make detailed plans.

"Oh, one more thing, Harry. Part of my job is to keep my ear to the ground. There's a lot of talk, and you'll hear it soon, about you running for office—governor or senator. The stories about your leadership in that little prehistoric town have gotten some politicos thinking, and the courage you showed this morning nailed it for me. As FBI Director, I shouldn't say this, but I think they have a wonderful idea."

CHAPTER THIRTY-NINE

I sat at my favorite New York spot, the restaurant at the Loeb Boathouse overlooking the lake in Central Park. Some of my wise guy fellow agents call it the Buster Boathouse. It takes a lot to calm my normally frenetic nerves, and the Loeb restaurant does the trick.

The temperature was perfect at 78 degrees with a gentle wind pushing the sailboats on the lake.

A tall nun approached my table, wearing the severe habit of the Dominican order. I noticed that she was wearing running shoes.

"Good afternoon young man. Care to join me in grace before meals?" Her voice was familiar, but I had a hard time placing it. She put a hand on my table, drew her face close to mine and said, "Hey, Bozo. It's me—Mike."

I spit my coffee across the table. As I was coughing, "Mike" sat down, adjusting his robes. Mike is famous among the few CIA agents who know him, for his disguises.

Mike, aka Muhammed Busharif, is the imam of a mosque in Brooklyn. Mike is six feet tall with the physique of a body builder, which he was for many years. He had to explain constantly to people in his mosque why he didn't wear a beard. He blamed it on a rare skin condition. Truth is, Mike simply didn't like beards. For most of his religious career, he quietly tended to the flock that worshipped at his mosque. But over time he became infuriated with all the terrorist killings in the name of his religion. When a good friend of his daughter was killed in a bomb attack at a football game, Mike went over the edge. He renounced his religion, but only to a select few people, including me. He became personal friends with Ayaan Hirsi Ali, the Muslim dissident and author. Besides Ali herself, I'm the only person who knows of his friendship with her. Mike's language tends to be earthy, not what you'd expect from a religious leader.

He's the most important mole the CIA ever had, and feeds us information that we could never get without an insider like him. In his mosque, Mike hears things that wouldn't faze a non-clergyman, including me, and I speak Arabic.

"Hey Sister Mike, nice robes, if somewhat dated," I said.

Mike laughed.

"I can't get an up-to-date wardrobe at garage sales," Mike said, "so put up with my datedness or increase my expense budget. To change the subject, I'm the one who usually calls meetings, Buster, so what's up, my friend?"

"Something big, Mike. Bigger than anything we ever discussed."

"Holy shit. Have you been taking drama lessons or are you shooting straight with me?"

"I never shoot anything but straight with you, Mike. I'll start by asking you a question: Have you heard about the *Maltese* and *Melody* incidents, the ship disappearances, and most recently, the *Ocean Magic*, which is still missing?"

"Of course. You can't own a TV or radio and not hear about them. Amazing stuff. Two ships disappear and then all the people suddenly come back after a couple of months in the distant past. And then another one vanishes off the coast of New Jersey. From what the pundits are saying, nobody knows how the events happened. Most people think it's a strange natural phenomenon."

"What do you think, Mike"

"I don't think there's anything natural about it. How the fuck can three ships simply disappear? No, Buster, I think there's a scumbag lurking in the shadows. Having said that, I don't know how somebody or some people could pull off an operation that makes a ship disappear."

"That's what I want to know," I said. "Who and how?"

"Am I stretching my imagination to say that you suspect a terrorist plot in the background?" Mike asked.

"No, Mike, your imagination is right on track. Every spook instinct in me says that these events are all part of a terrorist operation. We know this: at least two of the ships slipped through some sort of portal in the ocean, and the third ship probably did too, but half a world away. Most investigators call it a time portal, also known to time travel experts as a wormhole."

Mike knocked over his beer, spilling it on his robes.

"Holy shit, Buster, did you say a portal? The press has been using the word wormhole, but now that you mention it I recognize the word portal used on TV—and in my mosque."

"Do you think that people in your mosque may be just talking about the news reports?" I asked.

"Does the phrase, *Sacred Portal,* mean anything to you, Buster?"

"*Sacred Portal?* I found a piece of paper with those words on it above the coordinates of the wormhole. It was in the room of a guy who planned to kill one of the *Maltese* people. That phrase is mentioned in a radical book that's been circulating among jihadis. We found a copy in the guy's room."

I reached into my pocket and came out with an index card with notes on it, my favorite filing system.

"Here it is: 'Lure the infidel to the *Sacred Portal,* where he will be lost in time and space, never to return unless he finds the spot where the *Sacred Portal* was located.' Can you recall any context for that phrase, Mike?"

"I never thought about it, I'm embarrassed to admit," Mike said. "I remember people using it with the word *infidel.* I heard things like: 'The infidel will find himself lost in the *Sacred Portal.*' I didn't pay any attention to it. Some of my more radical congregants are always talking about infidels getting lost, just like they say *Great Satan* and the usual bullshit like that."

I flagged down the waitress to replace Mike's spilled beer.

"Buster, how the hell could somebody pull off something like that—a portal in the ocean that ships can pass through?"

"Beats me, Mike, but you just gave me something I've been looking for—a lead."

"Well, here's another one, Buster, but just like the first one I don't know what it means."

"Let's look for meaning later, Mike. Just tell me what you've heard."

"In the same conversations involving the *Sacred Portal*, I heard the word 'satellite' often. Hold on, let me get the cobwebs out of my brain. I heard sentences with the words, 'create, satellite, and *Sacred Portal*.' Is it possible that somebody's manufacturing these fucking things in space?"

"I don't know, Mike. Do you have the names of the men involved in these conversations?"

"Yes. One is Amir Muhammed and the other is Ali Moradi. Those are the only two I recall discussing a *Sacred Portal*."

"Do you know anything more about them, Mike?"

"Muhammed has been a member of my mosque for years. He's been pretty quiet until that new guy, Ali Moradi, joined. They're both aeronautical engineers. Muhammed works for an American company called Space Tech. It's a private company that manufactures and launches satellites. Moradi works for Northrup Grumman, the big American aerospace company, at their small New York office."

"How do you know so much about these guys, Mike?"

"Everybody who joins my mosque fills out a detailed form. Advanced terrorist security, no?"

"I think we both know what you'll be focused on in the near future, Mike."

"My ears are your ears, Buster."

"When I started this meeting I was in my own end zone trying to come up with a play," I said. "Now I'm 100 yards downfield and it's first and goal. You, Mike, are the best."

"Just give me the ball, my friend. I'll take it in for you."

CHAPTER FORTY

"So tell us, Mr. Super Spook, what's new?" Sarah Watson asked.

I sat with Sarah Watson and Bill Carlini in the conference room near Sarah's office. Dinosaur photos hung on the walls.

"I met yesterday with my favorite mole. As usual he almost drowned me with information."

"Buster, tell Sarah about Imam Mike," Bill Carlini said.

Although I hate to talk about a deep mole to anybody, especially somebody not from the CIA, my boss told me to bring Director Watson up to speed. I did, giving her Mike's background and a few cases he's helped us crack.

"I'm going to say two words and tell me what you think. '*Sacred Portal.*' Ring a bell?"

"Yes," both Sarah and Bill said. "It's in the record from Sarah's meeting a few days ago. That phrase was on a piece of paper you found in the room of that killer you told us about," Bill said. "It has something to do with hoping that infidels get lost in time. So, you heard more about the phrase?"

"I was talking to Imam Mike about the wormholes that are gobbling up American ships. He recalled two congregants from his mosque saying that phrase often. He also said that they used *Sacred Portal* in the same sentence as 'create' and 'satellite.' Both of those men are aeronautical engineers by trade. So, put your spook hats on. After I gave you that additional information, does *Sacred Portal* mean anything to you?"

"It could be the wormhole!" Watson yelled.

"Hey, remember, spooks don't yell. Bill, without yelling, tell me if you agree with Sarah."

"Yes, too coincidental to be an accident. It sounds like Imam Mike, as usual, is on to something. But how the hell can a human being create a wormhole?"

"We need to talk to our favorite scientist, Bob Flowers," I said.

***

On my suggestion, an agent met Bob Flowers at the building entrance and escorted him to Director Watson's office to be deputized as a federal agent. An accelerated background check had already been done on him.

"Hello again, Bob," I said. "I believe you've met CIA Director Carlini and, of course, FBI Director Watson."

"I heard all about Dinosaur Town from Buster," Carlini said. "An amazing story,"

"Actually, we called it Malta Town," Bob said, "but dinosaur town captures the spirit of the place. Do you mind if I ask a question? Why was I deputized just now as a federal agent?"

"That insures that you will spend a long time in prison if you divulge what we're talking about," Sarah Watson said.

"I guess I should be flattered," Bob said, wiping his forehead with a handkerchief.

"Buster tells us that you have a photographic memory," Carlini said. "How did that help you to get away from prehistoric times?"

"I never forget anything, but sometimes it takes me a while to drag the recollections from my brain. I remembered reading about wormholes in a physics textbook. At first, I didn't accept the idea of traveling through time, but I let the science occupy my mind rather than my opinions. That's when I pieced together our strange incident that propelled the *Maltese* back in time, and I realized it was a wormhole. The only thing that got in our way was our lack of fuel to get back to the wormhole location. When the

Melody of the Seas came upon us, I knew that she was our ticket home. Turns out, my theory was correct."

"Bob," I said, "did you ever consider the possibility that the wormhole could be man-made and not just an accident of nature?"

"I've toyed with the idea. Let me illustrate it for you."

Flowers walked over to a white board and wheeled it next to the conference table so we could see. He drew a circle representing earth, and a smaller one depicting a satellite.

"Satellites have been part of our world ever since the Russians launched *Sputnik* in 1957. We use them for everything from telecommunications, to space photography, to the GPS in our cars. With a powerful and sophisticated transmitter, it could place a mark on the earth. I don't understand the next part, but I can theorize that, given the right software, a satellite could be used to create a wormhole."

"Bob, I never mentioned a satellite. How did you come up with your theory?"

"You didn't need to mention a satellite, Buster. If you pose the idea of a man-made wormhole, the use of a satellite becomes immediately apparent. So, if you think someone or some group is behind these wormholes, who could it be?"

"Bob, it's obvious that we're thinking in that direction, but for now you don't have a 'need to know' just who we suspect."

"Ah yes, 'need to know,' the basic doctrine used to keep matters secret."

"I bet you're a killer at *Trivial Pursuit*," Watson said with a laugh.

"Well, let's just hope that what I'm pursuing isn't trivial."

CHAPTER FORTY-ONE

Meg and I put on our Navy uniforms for our trip into active duty. I looked in the mirror at the uniform on my slimmed down 2017 body.

"My God, Harry, if you had any more ribbons you'd need an extra chest. You look adorable in uniform."

"You don't look bad yourself, lieutenant," I said, "but then you'd look great in a potato sack. I'm still amazed that President Blake gave you a direct commission as a lieutenant. I never heard of such an action. Sarah Watson obviously impressed him with her stories about you."

We hitched a ride on a Navy cargo plane that was heading to the big Navy base in Norfolk, Virginia, which was the homeport of our ship. The Office of Naval Operations (NavOps) had picked out an experimental nuclear frigate, the *USS Davidson*, as the ship that would find and hopefully lead the *Ocean Magic* back to the present day. The only other nuclear vessels in the Navy were aircraft carriers and submarines. The *Davidson*, although considered experimental, was fully armed and operational, having taken its shakedown cruise already.

As we walked up the gangway, we heard the shrill sound of the bosun's pipe throughout the ship, followed by the announcement, "*Davidson*, arriving," the traditional Navy way to announce an arriving dignitary. The captain would always be announced by the name of the ship. So that's me—"*Davidson*." I would be lying if I said that I didn't feel nostalgia for my old Navy days. I told Meg to follow my lead with military formalities. When we got to the top of the gangway, I snapped a quick left-face and saluted the colors on the stern. Meg didn't know how to perform a military left-or-right-face, so she just turned to her left and gave a passable salute. Then we returned the salute of Lt. Jerry Higgins, the officer of the deck. We walked onto the quarterdeck, the traditional welcoming space on a Navy ship. Lieutenant Commander Jim McAteer, my executive officer, greeted us. A couple of sailors took our bags and showed us to our room. It was a typical small officer's room, but it had been outfitted with a double bed as I had ordered. This was not a typical Navy deployment, and everybody knew that Meg was my wife. My "sea cabin," the room I would occupy when we were underway, could only accommodate one person. Since we'd be underway constantly, I would sleep alone in my sea cabin the whole time.

"It's been a long time since we haven't slept together, honey," Meg said.

"That's all the more reason we need to find the *Ocean Magic* fast."

Jim McAteer, handled most of the details of getting the ship underway because he knew the ship well, having been the commanding officer during her shakedown cruise. As soon as our last line was cast off and the ship's horn sounded, a recording of *Anchors Aweigh*, the Navy theme song, played throughout the ship. Meg was standing next to me and snapped a picture.

"I couldn't pass up taking a photo of your face, Harry," Meg said. "When they played *Anchors Aweigh* I thought I saw a tear in your eye. Tell me you don't miss the Navy."

"I'll admit I do miss it," I said. "And the great thing about this command is that I get to serve with you next to me."

Just after we passed the breakwater to the ocean, Jim McAteer ordered the bosun's pipe sounded. He then made the announcement, "Attention all hands, attention all hands, stand by for Captain Harry Fenton."

"Good morning everyone," I said. "On behalf of my wife Lieutenant Meg and myself, I welcome all of you who volunteered for this mission, one of the weirdest operations the Navy has ever launched. I admire you for volunteering. You've heard and read what slipping through a wormhole is all about, and you know that I can't predict what we'll encounter. The last time Meg and I went through a wormhole we found ourselves on a dinosaur-infested island in the middle of nowhere. I don't expect that will happen again, but I have no idea what we'll encounter or what year we'll find ourselves in.

"Our job is to find the *Ocean Magic* and to lead her back through the wormhole to the present. We're four hours sailing time to the wormhole. I know you have all been briefed on this, but I'll review it again. We'll arrive at the coordinates of the wormhole at 1400 hours, which means we'll cross the portal in daylight. The sky will darken, and we'll feel a rumbling along our hull. After about two minutes, daylight will return, and we will emerge on the other side of the wormhole. Your briefing papers told you that we encountered prehistoric sharks. Whether that will happen again, I don't know. We'll make announcements as we get close to the coordinates. XO McAteer has requested that Meg and I give a talk in the mess hall about our experiences. So, in case any of you haven't' heard about our trip to the past on various TV shows, we'll be happy to answer any questions. Because we have a crew of only 75, everyone can fit in the mess hall. If you're not on watch, please join us."

***

Meg and I had a great time recounting our 10 years in Malta Town to our crew of about-to-be time travelers. We brought with us a briefcase full of photos. We then asked if anybody had any questions.

Chief Petty Officer, Joseph Croner raised his hand.

"Captain, what if we can't find the *Ocean Magic?* Are we going to abandon the search after a set amount of time?"

"Chief, I've set a time limit of one-month of 2017 time based on our ship's chronometer. After a month, I'm going to put it to a vote. I know that sounds strange coming from the captain of a Navy ship, but this is a unique mission. I'm not about to keep you folks away from your families indefinitely."

XO McAteer stood. "Captain, it's a half hour to the wormhole coordinates."

"Okay everybody," I said, "you're about to experience the strangest trip of your lives. A couple of things to keep in mind. This is a ship of the

United States Navy, and we're all Navy people. Although our mission is to find the cruise ship, I'm treating this as a military operation, including gunnery drills. I have a reputation as a hard ass, so be prepared to work. As we approach the wormhole, I'm going to order general quarters. Because we don't know what to expect, I want everybody at their battle stations. That is all. Carry on."

The shrill sound of the bosun's pipe sounded, followed by a clanging bell, "General quarters, general quarters, all hands man your battle stations. This is not a drill. I repeat, this is not a drill."

Meg and I went to the bridge, along with Jim McAteer. I put a helmet on Meg's head and cinched the strap under her chin.

"What the hell is this for?" Meg asked.

"We all wear helmets at our battle stations, hon—in case we go into battle. Here, put this life jacket on too."

Jim read the countdown over the PA system. "Zero minus 10 seconds, nine…three, two, one, we're on the target."

The bright daylight disappeared, the sky became pitch black, and the hull started to rumble. After two minutes, as we expected, the daylight returned. We were…wherever the hell we were. As we had drilled, McAteer took an immediate electronic fix from our inertial navigation system. Like most ships, the *Davidson* had a readout monitor on the bridge that kept a running fix from both the GPS plotter and the inertial navigation tracker, also known as a dead reckoning or DR tracker, which records every movement of the ship. The GPS was inoperable, confirming our assumption that we were in a different era of time.

The bosun's pipe sounded again.

"Attention all hands, attention all hands, stand by for Captain Fenton."

"Well, we've done it, people, we've passed through a wormhole, and you are now officially time travelers. Expect to be invited to a lot of cocktail parties. We have no idea what year we're in, but our lack of satellites tells us that we're in the past. We're going to secure from general quarters in a few minutes, and then begin our hunt for the *Ocean Magic.*"

"My hair's going to be a mess," Meg said, peering at me from under her helmet.

"Look at it this way, Meg. Your hair's a mess every time we make love. I think it looks cute."

"This is not my idea of sex, captain," Meg whispered.

I handed her the radio. She had practiced radio calls, so I figured she would be the voice of The *USS Davidson.*

"*Ocean Magic, Ocean Magic* this is Navy ship *USS Davidson*, come in." Meg said, sounding like a salty pro. Normally we would give our radio code name, *Lima Foxtrot*, but we didn't expect any other ships besides the *Ocean Magic.*

"*Ocean Magic, Ocean Magic* this is Navy ship *USS Davidson*, come in."

"*Ocean Magic, Ocean Magic* this is Navy ship *USS Davidson*, come in."

"We don't know which way the *Ocean Magic* went after it came through the wormhole," I said, "and we may be out of range."

"Captain, this ship is equipped with the most sophisticated radio in the fleet," Jim McAteer said. "Since both ships transmit and receive from the top of our antennas, the range can be as high as 40 nautical miles. We don't know which way the *Ocean Magic* will be heading, of course, so it may be hours or days before they're within radio range."

"Launch drone one, Jim," I said.

"Aye, aye, captain. I'll make sure drone two is ready to fly," McAteer said.

The *Davidson* was armed with two of the most sophisticated new drones. Manufactured by Northrup Grumman, the craft can take off and land vertically and sweep into a fixed-wing contour in flight. It's called a TERN, short for the catchy title, *Tactically Exploited Reconnaissance Node.* With a range of 975 miles, the drones are ideal for our search-and-rescue mission. I ordered the drone to fly at 30,000 feet, giving it a wide view of the ocean below, and hopefully, a moving cruise ship.

After two hours of scanning the ocean, the drone picked up not one, but four ships steaming on a northeasterly course, about 10 miles from our current location. I ordered the drone pilot to drop down in altitude for a better look.

"Do you see the insignia on the aft deck of the lead ship, captain?" Jim McAteer asked, looking at the video repeater in front of him.

"It's the war insignia of the Kriegsmarine, the German Navy in World War II," I said. "I guess we know approximately what era we're in, either the 1930s or 1940s. The ship behind the formation is a cruise ship, no doubt the *Ocean Magic* judging from the Royal Caribbean emblem on her foredeck. The warships include one heavy cruiser and two destroyers. I'm going to use the long-range radio with a modern frequency those German ships can't monitor."

"*Ocean Magic, Ocean Magic*, this is the United States Navy ship, *USS Davidson*," Meg said into the microphone.

"Read you loud and clear, *Davidson*. This is Captain Dereck Burton of the *Ocean Magic*. God bless you. I can see your drone overhead from the bridge."

I grabbed the radio.

"Captain Burton, this is Captain Harry Fenton of the *Davidson*. We took a trip through the wormhole and came looking for you folks. I guess by now you've figured out that you've traveled through time. Apparently, it didn't occur to you to retrace your steps and cross back over the wormhole, which is exactly what we intend to do, but first I have a couple of big questions. First, what year are we in and what's going on with those Nazi ships in front of you? Speak freely because those ships can't monitor this radio frequency."

"Captain Fenton, we're in the year 1942 and are very much at war with the bastards in front of us. Please have your drone focus on the stern of my ship and you'll see just how much of a war we're in."

"Looks like artillery damage to me, Captain Burton."

"That's exactly what you're looking at. I tried to communicate with the captain of their lead cruiser, but the son-of-a-bitch fired his guns at us without answering. 49 of our passengers have been killed. Our stern thrusters are inoperable, but our main engines are okay as well as our propellers. He then told me, through a translator, that we're being led to Bremerhaven, about 300 miles from our current position. My ship will be impounded and all of us will be held as prisoners of war. Are you going to try to negotiate with them captain?"

"Negotiate? That did *you* a hell of a lot of good. No, I'm going to teach those bastards a few lessons on modern naval warfare. Order all of you people to stay inboard and away from windows. It's going to get nasty and noisy around here shortly."

I looked at Jim McAteer, my XO. His face was as white as snow. From the background I read about him, he'd never seen combat. He was about to experience it.

"Jim, sound general quarters. Helmsman steer course 060. Engine room, this is the bridge. All engines ahead full."

"General quarters, general quarters, all hands man your battle stations. This is not a drill. I repeat, this is not a drill."

"Harry, what's going on?" Meg asked as she donned her helmet.

"We're going to blow up some Nazis."

Meg slammed a new magazine into her 45.

"We'll be using some bigger ammo than that, hon. Let's go to CIC."

"What's CIC, Harry? Don't speak jargon."

"It's the Combat Information Center. It's where we go to kill the enemy. I'm going to make an announcement to the crew."

"Attention all hands, attention all hands, stand by for Captain Fenton."

"This is Captain Fenton speaking. Well, we've found the *Ocean Magic* and we're in the year 1942. The *Ocean Magic* is being escorted by three German warships, after one of the ships fired on her, killing 49 passengers. So, we find ourselves at war, and we're about to rain hell on the Nazis. Stand by and keep your ears open for further announcements."

We could see the *Ocean Magic* and her captors on the horizon. The Nazis were about to get the surprise of their lives. I pressed the button for Battery One, the missile station where we keep our anti-ship Harpoon missiles.

"Battery one, prepare to fire on my command. Fix your targets from the drone's radar. Take out the first ship, a heavy cruiser, then work back but avoid the large cruise ship, which is the *Ocean Magic.*"

"Battery One prepared to launch, captain."

"Fire one."

The *Davidson* shuddered as the Harpoon took off.

The Harpoon anti-ship missile is 12.6 feet long, 13.5 inches in diameter, and weighs 1,523 pounds. The warhead alone weighs 488 pounds. It's designed to penetrate the hull of an enemy vessel and detonate inside the ship. Depending on where it penetrated, one Harpoon missile can sink a ship.

We could see the action on the video feed from the drone, which told me that our first strike was successful. The mid-section of the heavy cruiser exploded with such force, I guessed we hit the ship's ammunition magazine. The ship sank in two parts. I ordered two more strikes against the destroyers. One of them sank immediately, and the other drifted aimlessly and then disappeared beneath the waves.

Meg was standing next to me in CIC. She looked up at me, her helmet tilted slightly askew on her head.

"You're such a gentle person, Harry. I can't believe what I just saw."

"I'm not gentle with the enemy, hon, and they are definitely the enemy. The commander of the Nazi flotilla made that clear by firing on a defenseless cruise ship."

"*Ocean Magic, Ocean Magic*, this is *USS Davidson*."

"Read you loud and clear, Captain Fenton. I can't believe you sank the entire Nazi flotilla. I can see you on the horizon. Is there a fleet behind you??"

"No, just one ship, Captain Burton, one ship with a lot of fire power. When we get close to your position, you'll follow the *Davidson* to the wormhole, about 550 miles from your current location. I want you to immediately lower at least three of your passenger launches and as many life rafts as you can fit in them. There will be survivors floating around, and we want to give them a chance. After I hammer the enemy, I always throw him a lifeline. It's only right."

I felt the same as I did when I took my little cousin Billy home.

In a few minutes we closed on the *Ocean Magic's* position. I told Captain Burton to position his ship 100 yards off our stern. We were set to cross the wormhole at three in the afternoon, or 1500 hours.

Meg counted down to the wormhole spot. "Zero minus five, four, three, two, one. We're on the target, honey, I mean Harry, I mean captain. Hey, I'm not used to this military shit."

We got what we expected, what we hoped for. The daylight turned dark, the hull rumbled and two minutes later we were in daylight. A quick check of our GPS told me we were back in 2017. Sailors hunched over the rails on both sides of the ship looking aft to see if the *Ocean Magic* made it. Perfect. She was steaming right behind us. My entire crew erupted in cheers.

My orders were to escort the ship to its dock at Port Liberty, New Jersey. I waited for the *Ocean Magic* to tie up. She required the assistance of two tugboats, because the artillery attack damaged her stern thrusters.

At least her main engines and propellers were okay. I eased the *Davidson* next to the open dock behind her. The pier was packed with family and friends of both ships. My cell phone rang.

"Harry, it's Sarah Watson. I'm wearing a yellow suit and I'm standing lined up with your bridge. A car is waiting to take you, Meg, and LCDR McAteer to Federal Plaza for, you guessed it, a debriefing. I have another car waiting to bring Captain Burton of the *Ocean Magic*. Burton told me all about your actions, Harry. You've done it again, my friend. Mission accomplished."

***

We had just entered the conference room when the intercom sounded.

"It's the White House on line one, Director Watson. The president says that he wants to speak to Captain Fenton."

Holy shit, I thought. The president wants to speak to me?

Meg and I walked into the hallway to take the call.

"Yes, sir, Mr. President, Harry Fenton here."

"Harry, you're quite a guy. From everything I've read and heard about you, you performed just as we expected. From your heroism on that destroyer in the Gulf, to your leadership of your crew and passengers when you were lost in another time, to this latest action of yours, rescuing the *Ocean Magic*, you have once again shown yourself to be a great American. I was going to have my chief of staff call you, but I wanted to talk to you myself. Please come to the White House next Friday, where I will award you your second Navy Cross."

I thought I would faint. Instead I shot off my mouth.

"I'm honored, Mr. President, but I must say something. Except for my actions in the Navy, there's another person without whom I could not have accomplished any of those other things. You can ask anyone involved in any of those operations and they'd agree. That would be my wife, Meghan Fenton."

"Harry, I've heard all about your wonderful wife and partner. I would be remiss if I didn't honor her as well. Here's what I'm going to do. At the same time I award you your second Navy Cross, I will award Meghan her first. From everything I've heard, she deserves it. Oh, and another thing. I'm promoting you to the rank of rear admiral, effective immediately. I've already cleared it with the Navy brass. They can be pains in the ass, but I got nothing but enthusiasm for the idea of promoting you. I'm not requiring it, but I hope you will decide to stay in the Navy. We need people like you."

When I hung up the phone, Meg wrapped her arms around me.

"Do I have to call you Admiral Harry from now on?"

"You can still call me Harry, but now that I'm an admiral, please don't call me Dickbrain."

CHAPTER FORTY-TWO

"Buster, it's Mike. You won't believe this but there's a high-level meeting going on in a conference room at my mosque. Three guys are here, including a technical honcho named Mahmood Khan. A lot of what they're saying is scientific stuff that I don't understand, but they're talking in detail about using a satellite to create a *Sacred Portal.*"

"Mike, can you record what they're saying?"

"Buster, do you think I'm stupid? I've recorded every word in two recordings. Here's one spot that I marked. Listen to this:"

"The infidels cannot escape the *Sacred Portal.* First, we will send them to another time, then we will kill them."

"That's it Mike, a threat of death. It's enough evidence to arrest them. I'll be there in 20 minutes with my FBI friends."

"Better hurry up, Buster. I think their conversation is winding down."

"Do whatever you need to do to slow them down, Mike. I'm at Federal Plaza, not far from your mosque in Brooklyn. We should be there shortly."

"Good afternoon, gentlemen," Mike said to the three men in Arabic. "It's always a pleasure to see someone new at my mosque. And who, may I ask, is this gentleman?" Mike said, gesturing toward Mahmood Khan.

"He is Mohmar Alsavi, Imam Bushariff," one of the men said, making up a fictitious name for Khan.

"It is my pleasure to meet you, Imam. We were just about to leave." Khan said.

"Please, gentlemen, be my guests for lunch. I will order food brought here to the conference room," Mike said as he felt for the gun under his robe.

"No, thank you for your hospitality, Imam, but we must leave."

"Stay put," Mike shouted in English as he chambered a round and pointed his Glock at them.

"Imam, you have three guests," his assistant said over the intercom.

Buster, along with three FBI agents rushed into the room with their guns drawn. They handcuffed each of the men. Four more FBI agents came into the room to escort the men to a waiting government van.

***

Two days later, Buster and Imam Mike spoke on a secure phone.

"Thanks to you, Mike, I'm sure we got them all. They gave up the name of the CEO at the American company that launches civilian satellites and we've got him in custody too. Our scientific people questioned them non-stop about how they managed to pull off the *Sacred Portal*. We now know the secrets."

"I'm amazed that they spoke so openly. They didn't ask to see a lawyer?"

"I can be very persuasive when I need to, Mike. Come to my office later at six. We're going to have a little celebration. After Captain Harry Fenton's rescue mission of the *Ocean Magic*, and because of your actions, I'm happy to announce that The *Sacred Portal* conspiracy is officially dead."

CHAPTER FORTY-THREE

Lieutenant Joseph Sprague banked his EA-18G Growler warplane to the left as he prepared to land on his ship, the *USS Gerald R. Ford*. The *Ford* had recently been commissioned, and it will be more than two years before it's deployed overseas. It's the first aircraft carrier in the new *Ford* class of ships destined to replace the aging *Nimitz* class carriers. The *Ford*'s home port is the huge Naval Station Norfolk in Virginia.

The *USS Gerald R. Ford* is a large ship, over 1,100 feet in length with a beam of 134 feet. She displaces over 100,000 tons and carries a complement of 4,660 people. Her range, with her two nuclear reactors, is virtually unlimited. She can cruise for 20 to 25 years, her time at sea limited only by the needs of the crew and routine maintenance.

Sprague, having earned his wings five years earlier, loves to fly, especially his newest jet, the EA-18G Growler. The plane is a specialized version of the F/A-18 Super Hornet. Despite his affection for flying, there is one maneuver he dreads, although he'll never admit it—landing on a carrier deck. Although the *Ford* is a gigantic ship, to a pilot coming in for a landing it looks like a toy in the ocean.

One of the pilot's most critical jobs is to "call the ball," indicating to the landing crew on the ship's flight deck that he has a visually accurate view of the "meatball." The ball, or meatball, is an orange orb of light emitted from the optical landing system on the carrier's flight deck. A green horizontal row of lights (known as the datum) indicates proper glide slope. If the ball is below the datum, the aircraft is low, and if it's above the datum, the aircraft is high. When the ball is in proper view, the pilot says, "Roger Ball."

As his plane approached the *Ford*, Sprague called out "Roger Ball, Roger Ball, Roger Ball...Holy Shit!"

As the *Ford* bathed in the afternoon sun, a dark cloud enveloped it. Sprague had the ball in clear view, but then it was gone—gone, along with the ship. Instinctively he circled the spot of ocean where he last saw the *Ford*. After a couple of minutes, the dark cloud disappeared, and the sunshine resumed, but the ship wasn't there, only a smooth ocean. Because his flight was the last scheduled to land, Sprague couldn't communicate with other aircraft. He was alone.

He turned his plane toward shore and looked at his fuel indicator. He calculated that Naval Station Norfolk was 75 miles from his position, and that he had enough fuel to make it. His mind a complete jumble, he couldn't remember his call sign code, nor that of the Naval Base.

"Alpha Bravo, Alpha Bravo, this is Charlie Sierra," or some shit like that, he thought. Then he decided to go for simple English.

"Naval Station Norfolk, Naval Station Norfolk, this is Lieutenant Sprague in flight 209 from the *USS Gerald R. Ford*, come in please."

"Read you, lieutenant. We can't communicate with the *Ford*. Do you have any idea what happened?"

"The fucking ship disappeared on me as I was about to land," Sprague shouted. "Your guess is as good as mine."

"Hey, Joe, this is Commander Jim Luce. You're up for promotion to lieutenant commander in a couple of months. Watch your language."

"Commander Jim, I repeat, the fucking ship disappeared," Sprague said. "I don't give a shit about my language. The *Ford* is simply not there."

"You're cleared for landing, Joe. Calm down first."

***

Meg and I were in second floor conference room at 26 Federal Plaza, down the hall from in Sarah Watson's New York office. We had completed another session of debriefing the *Ocean Magic* mission. Buster from the CIA and a couple of FBI agents were there with us, waiting for

Sarah Watson. As Sarah had requested, Meg and I wore our Navy uniforms, mine sporting my new admiral's stripes. We were about to lift a few rounds to celebrate the good news. Sarah and Meg had struck up a friendship in the past few days. I think she befriended Meg because she likes to hang around people with brains and a sense of humor. The spooks were still interested in talking to us about our adventure, even though the wormhole problem was dead and gone. They wanted to know all about how a group of a thousand people could carve out a working town in a prehistoric forest.

"Hey, guys, Director Watson is on the line," The receptionist said.

Buster walked over to the speaker and pressed the button.

"We're all here. Go ahead, Sarah."

"I just got a call from the White House, folks. Turn on the TV. We lost a carrier, the USS *Gerald R. Ford*, off the coast of Virginia—not the Azores, not New Jersey—Virginia. The ship was just commissioned a few days ago. A pilot who was about to land reported that the ship simply disappeared from sight and from radar. He also described a strange darkness that suddenly enshrouded the ship for a couple of minutes. Sound familiar?"

Not a word was said in the conference room. Not even from me. Or Meg. Or Buster.

"Hey, Buster," Watson said, "I just got an email in Arabic. I'll forward it to you. Please translate it for us."

Buster turned on his phone, and then clicked on the message he just got from Sarah Watson.

Buster read the message.

"Stay where you are, infidels. Don't move. Your next step may take you through a *Sacred Portal*."

CHARACTERS – THE MALTESE INCIDENT

Abdul, Raman – Imposter and spy, aka Jason Thomas

Akhbar, Gamal – aka Buster, CIA Agent

Burton, Dereck – Captain of the *Ocean Magic*

Ciano, Dennis – Master at Arms on the *Melody of the Seas*

Atkins, George – *See* Akhbar, Gamal

Avila, Alfonso – Portuguese boatyard owner

Bellino, Wally – Construction expert

Borg, Randolph – CEO, Malta Investment Company

Buster – Aka Gamal Akhbar – CIA Agent

Carlini, William – Director, CIA

Donaldson, George – Electrical engineer

Fenton, Harry – Captain of the *Maltese*

Feigenbaum, Max - Paleontologist

Fletcher, Mike – Maritime investigator

Flowers, Bob - Chief Science Advisor for Malta Investment Company

Flynn, Rebecca – Chief Judge of Malta Town

Johnson, Meghan – VP of Operations for Malta Investment Company

Kahn, Abdul – Inventor and terrorist

Langdon, James – Captain, *USS Forrest Sherman*

MacCallum, Martha – TV anchor and reporter

Maslow, Dominic – Head of shore party from the *Maltese*.

McAteer, James – Executive Officer, *USS Davidson*

Moradi, Ali – Terrorist operative.

Muhammed, Amir – Terrorist operative.

Murphy, Frank – Securities analyst and dinosaur expert

Morgan, Joseph – Philanthropist to radical Islamist causes.

Orlando, William – Head of legislative committee of Malta Town

Ragnarssen, Lars – Captain of the *Melody of the Seas*

Simmons, Bob – First Officer on the *Melody of the Seas*

Thomas, Jason - Spy

Truesdale, Jamal – Chief of Police of Malta Town

Valente, James – First Officer on the *Maltese*

THE BOOKS OF RUSS MORAN

All books are available on Amazon.com, and also as ebooks on The Kindle or a Kindle app on your smartphone or iPad.

The Gray Ship – Book One of The Time Magnet Series

http://amzn.to/16GPumH

"This provocative, intensely powerful novel is a must-read for sci-fi fans and Civil War aficionados, though mainstream fiction readers will find it heart-rending and inspiring as well. A rare read that's not only wildly entertaining, but also profoundly moving." — Kirkus Reviews

The Thanksgiving Gang – Book Two of The Time Magnet Series

http://amzn.to/1NzBs7N

"I had never read a book before written in an efficient, minimalistic prose. Instead of writing what most readers want to read, he gives voice to life-like characters, with their flaws and prejudices. They are not infallible superheroes. It's always nice to find a new voice in fiction and to enjoy creativity at its best." — C. Ludewig. "Breakneck pacing and virtually nonstop action" – Kirkus Reviews

A Time of Fear – Book Three of The Time Magnet Series

http://amzn.to/1zdjaG9

"His story is fascinating, and adds even more depth to this already cavernously deep novel. Amazingly unique, chilling and well written, Moran weaves a future that is both desperate and hopeful. Blending modern fears with science fiction results in a tale that will keep you reading long into the night." Five stars!" —Heather

The Skies of Time – Book Four of The Time Magnet Series

http://amzn.to/1CCC3jg

In *The Skies of Time*, you will recognize the two main characters, Ashley Patterson, now an admiral, and her husband, Jack Thurber. They met and fell in love in *The Gray Ship*, and now they're in for the adventure of their lives in *The Skies of Time*. Ashley and Jack have been such prominent characters in all four books of The Time Magnet Series that I feel like they're old friends. You will also recognize some of the other characters. But if I told you who they are, it would ruin the fun.

"I'm big fan of this series and this one may be the best. I hope there is another book to this series since it keeps getting better. There are a few questions I have about certain events that makes the next one even more suspenseful. These are great books to binge read one after the other." — Time Travel Fan

The Shadows of Terror – Book One of the Patterns Series

http://amzn.to/1IDQzJS

A novel that explodes off the front page of your newspaper.

Terrorism has a new face, a face that's obscured in the shadows. The radical forces of destruction have learned to make themselves invisible to the West, and preventing a terrorist attack has become almost impossible.

A new war has begun, World War III.

Rick Bellamy, an FBI agent who specializes in counterterrorism, is engaged in his own war, a war with no end.

Bellamy's wife, Ellen, a prominent architect, discovers that she's in the middle of the greatest terror plot to date.

To defeat the enemy, Bellamy first has to uncover the clues, to shine a light on the shadows. He has to find patterns – before it's too late.

"Move over James Patterson and Mary Higgins Clark. There's a new guy in town. Russ Moran's new book – *The Shadows of Terror.*" — Frank from Lynbrook

The Scent of Revenge - Book Two in the Patterns Series.

http://amzn.to/1UvDRmw

The world is at war with the forces of terror. FBI Agent Rick Bellamy and his wife, Ellen, find themselves in the middle of a sinister terrorist plot.

Someone is attacking young prominent women, inflicting a horrible disease.

Nobody knows its origin, nobody knows how to stop it, nobody knows how to cure it.

Rick Bellamy and a team of scientists want to go on the offense. But how?

Will the lives of the women be changed forever? When will the attacks stop?

"Heart pounding, can't put down thriller that will force you to look at terrorism in different light. Life in America will never be the same." — Cold Coffee Cafe

Sideswiped - Book One in the Matt Blake series of legal thrillers.

http://amzn.to/1MkxX35

Trial lawyer Matt Blake took on a perfect case.

It involved a sideswipe collision in which his client's husband, an investigative reporter, was killed. The evidence of negligence was overwhelming. Eyewitnesses testified that defendant was talking on his cell phone when he hit the other car.

But was it negligence? Was it an accident?

Or was it murder?

Matt uncovers evidence that the act may have been intentional. Somebody wanted the man silenced. Somebody wanted the man dead.

Somebody had a lot to hide.

The signs started to point to the highest levels of government.

An open-and-shut personal injury case suddenly became a vast conspiracy of terror.

"This book hooks you in from the first line. *Sideswiped* draws you into the world of Matt Blake and you become emotionally attached to him and his journey. The story itself is so well-written and moves quickly there is never a dull moment." —Sarah Elle

"Moran demonstrates the depth of his writing talent by developing a new genre with *Sideswiped*, a legal thriller. Branching out from his previous novels dealing with time travel, Moran goes in a whole new direction with Book One in the Matt Blake series. He creates a wild but totally believable story of modern day intrigue and suspense. Moran also deftly weaves into this book some of my favorite characters from his prior novels. I am looking forward to starting Book #2 - *The Reformers* — Frank from Lynbrook on August 16, 2016

The Reformers - Book Two of the Matt Blake series of legal thrillers, is the sequel to Sideswiped.

http://amzn.to/2m8uMdu

The forces of radical Islam are on the run.

Their leadership has been decimated, their ranks thinned, their power disappearing by the week.

Their recruiting efforts have been cut off, the radical websites shut down, and the attraction of jihad is losing its appeal among the young.

With targeted assassinations, military strikes, as well as the loss of oil fields and gold mines, radical Islam is fast losing power.

But who is responsible?

It isn't the United States Government. It's a new force the world has never seen before.

Lawyer Matt Blake and his wife Diana find themselves in the middle of the most gigantic plot the world has ever seen, a conspiracy that's only begun to grow.

"I've been a fan of the author, Russell Moran, since reading *Sideswiped* a few months ago, so I admittedly went into this book with quite high expectations. That being said, I had no idea that *"The Reformers"* was going to play out in the way that it does and I can see myself giving this book a re-read in the future. In fact, I am even more impressed by the storyline of this read than the last and it has left me excited to see more." Lucidity.

The Keepers of Time – Book Five of the Time Magnet Series

http://amzn.to/2wjVSTt

Admiral Ashley Patterson and her husband Jack have done it again. They've traveled through time, 200 years into the future—aboard a nuclear aircraft carrier, Ashley's flagship.

They discover a new world, a strange new world—a post-nuclear war world—one that is both a beacon of hope, and a cry of despair.

They meet a group of people who call themselves *The Keepers of Time,* an organization dedicated to preserving history and culture amid the horrors of a dystopian future.

The world around them has harkened back to a primitive and savage past, one that includes human sacrifice.

Ashley knows they must have to get back to the present to warn the government of the unspeakable horrors that await.

But finding the way back to the present is their greatest challenge, an almost insurmountable one.

"A wild time travel yarn that starts fast and doesn't slow down until the end."

A Reunion in Time

http://amzn.to/2tneIsg

What if a 37-year-old adult travels back 20 years in time and finds himself in high school, followed by his 36-year-old wife? They're now teenagers, 17 and 16.

Adults in teenage bodies, they struggle to convince the people from their past that they are real, not apparitions. With the benefit of hindsight, they know the history of the past 20 years, and it isn't pretty.

Rick and Ellen are married, and now have to adjust to married life as teenagers in 2001. Rick is a senior FBI official and Ellen is a famous architect.

But everybody sees them as kids. Nobody believes that they're married, and nobody believes their stories—until Rick and Ellen predict 9/11.

How do they find their way back to the year they came from? How do they warn the authorities of the cataclysm that will occur in the future? The answer is to find the time portal—the wormhole—that brought them to 2001. But the site has changed. It's no longer the place where they crossed the wormhole. Will they live out the balance of their lives beginning as teenagers? "We've all wish we could go back to earlier times with the mind we have now. This Russell Moran book takes you there and it is a fun creative romp well worth reading. *A Reunion in Time* is highly recommend!" Kindle Customer.

The President is Missing – Book Three of the Matt Blake series.

http://amzn.to/2t9v7wu

While he was addressing the nation from a submerged nuclear submarine, President Blake's message is suddenly cut off. Anyone listening heard an explosion. The explosion was followed by floating debris five minutes later.

First Lady Dee Blake has doubts, which she shares with naval high command and the new president. She thinks the explosion and the debris were a ruse to make people think the sub was destroyed, and her husband with it.

Could the sub have been hijacked and the president kidnapped?

But who would commit such an act? What is its purpose?

Was it Russia, China, Iran, or a shadowy group of freelance terrorists?

The new president appoints Dee as his Chief of Staff, with explicit instructions to find the missing submarine—and President Matt Blake.

Her life, and the life of the nation, suddenly take a horrifying turn.

Robot Depot

http://amzn.to/2zXW7C2

Mike Bateman is a visionary businessman, the creator and CEO of the fabulously successful chain of stores, Robot Depot, a company dedicated to selling robots and Artificial Intelligence machines for a variety of uses.

The company is a darling of Wall Street and is the most popular destination for consumers and businesses looking for labor saving devices.

But the company caught the eye of ISIS, the terrorist Islamic State. They discover a great way to deliver bombs – using the products of Robot Depot to kill people.

Robot Depot changed from being a popular company to an object of fear because of the tampered products it sells. The terrorists use the company for "terror spectaculars," including the destruction of a skyscraper, a drone attack on Yankee Stadium, and the bombing of a children's sailing regatta.

Mike Bateman and the FBI are in a race to stop his products from becoming weapons, a race to stop the wanton killings. His wife and partner, Jenny, discovers the true meaning of terror one horrible summer day.

A Climate of Doubt

A book that looks at the horrors of climate change, and how it became a weapon of terrorism, was published in May of 2018. It's Book Four of the Matt Blake Series. Matt and Dee Blake take on their biggest challenge to date, along with our old friends, Rick and Ellen Bellamy.

If you enjoyed *The Maltese Incident*, please consider leaving a brief review on amazon.com. Reviews are an author's lifeblood.

ABOUT THE AUTHOR

In addition to the 14 novels discussed above, I also published five nonfiction books: *Justice in America: How it Works—How it Fails; The APT Principle: The Business Plan That You Carry in Your Head; Boating Basics: The Boattalk Book of Boating Tips; If You're Injured: A Consumer Guide to Personal Injury Law; How to Create More Time.* I'm a lawyer and a veteran of the United States Navy. I live on Long Island, New York, with my wife and editor, Lynda.

www.ingramcontent.com/pod-product-compliance
Lightning Source LLC
Chambersburg PA
CBHW070123260626
47160CB00004B/1590